VICTORIAN MANSION FLOWER SHOP MYSTERIES

Loot of All Evil

Elizabeth Penney

AnniesFiction.com

Books in the Flower Shop Mysteries series

Library of Congress-in-Publication Data
Loot of All Evil / by Elizabeth Penney
p. cm.
I. Title
                          2018933092

AnniesFiction.com
(800) 282-6643
Victorian Mansion Flower Shop Mysteries™
Series Creators: Shari Lohner, Janice Tate
Editor: Elizabeth Morrissey
Cover Illustrator: Bob Kayganich

10 11 12 13 14 | Printed in China | 9 8 7 6 5 4 3 2 1

1

One sunny November morning on Washington's Orcas Island, Kaylee Bleu opened the front door of her florist shop, The Flower Patch, and stepped into a thicket of . . . pumpkins?

Arrangements made with white, orange, frosted, and gilded miniature pumpkins caught her eye from every surface. Pumpkin-trimmed garlands were tacked to the Victorian mansion's ornate window and door trim, and vibrant matching wreaths hung on the wall. A giant basket full of speckled pumpkins trimmed in bittersweet vines rested near the front counter, and pint-size cuties marched along the countertop. Although she was a botanist by training, Kaylee hadn't realized that the *Cucurbita pepo* family had so many varied and tiny forms. Even her dachshund, Bear, seemed impressed as he glanced around with wide eyes.

"What do you think?" Mary Bishop grinned, blue eyes twinkling behind her glasses. The part-time floral designer had stayed on when Kaylee bought her grandmother's shop, and Kaylee was forever grateful. Mary's brilliant, innovative designs never failed to delight.

She must have been up all night doing this.

Kaylee set down her tote, her gaze still taking in the colorful displays. "I love them. They're gorgeous. But I thought pumpkin season was over. Well, except for pie at Thanksgiving dinner."

Mary nodded. "That's how it used to be, when everyone grew jack-o'-lanterns or pie pumpkins. But these ornamental types have really caught on. I thought we could do a big push with them for late fall this year, if you like the idea." She touched a pale-green eucalyptus wreath adorned with vibrant mini pumpkins. "We can sell wreaths like this all the way through Christmas."

"I think it's a great idea, Mary." Kaylee's brain began to whirl with design ideas of her own. *Pumpkins: not just for Halloween anymore.* She smiled.

Bear sniffed at a snowman created from stacked white pumpkins and gave a little bark, making the women laugh. "We'll put that snowman in the back until after Thanksgiving," Mary said. "I know some stores put out Christmas stuff in mid-November or earlier, but I'm not quite ready for that."

"Me neither." Kaylee sighed, thinking of the holiday fast approaching. With her parents in Florida and her grandmother in Arizona, it was shaping up to be another quiet one in her small adopted hometown of Turtle Cove. "I can't believe Thanksgiving is only two weeks away. Where does the time go?"

Mary ran a hand through her white and gray bob. "Wait until you're my age. The months and years really seem to zip by."

"That's what Grandma always says." Kaylee started walking toward the back, where there was a small kitchen. "Want some coffee? I need another cup this morning."

"Yes please," Mary called. "I'm going to get this place straightened up before we open."

By the time Kaylee returned with two coffee mugs, Jessica Roberts, owner of Death by Chocolate, the bakery next door, was at the counter talking to Mary. "These pumpkins are adorable." Jessica picked up two of the smallest, one perfectly round and the other with white ribs and orange stripes. "What are they, babies?" Petite with short, dark hair, the baker's pretty features revealed her Asian heritage.

"No, they're bred to be small," Mary said. "And in different colors too. Every year there are new varieties coming out."

"Consider me a fan." Jessica gently set the pumpkins back

on the counter, then clasped her hands together. "I've come to ask you both for a favor." With a slight wince, she waited for an answer.

"What is it, Jess?" Kaylee asked as she settled on a stool behind the counter. Jessica was known for her enthusiastic overcommitment at times, so Kaylee had a pretty good idea where this was going.

Jessica's bright eyes danced between their faces. "As you know, I'm on the planning committee for the Turtle Cove community Thanksgiving dinner this year. It's going to be held at the Northern Lights Inn, which is a fantastic location. We're getting donations of locally grown vegetables and even turkeys raised here on the island—"

Kaylee grinned. "And you need some volunteers. Well, count me in. I won't be with family, so helping with the community dinner sounds perfect." Even she could hear the dejection in her voice.

"Bea's not coming?" Jessica asked. "I'm sorry to hear that. And I take it you're not going to see her or your parents either?"

"No, not this year." Kaylee pretended great interest in her coffee, which wasn't nearly as good as the fresh-ground java Jessica brewed next door. "But I'm sure a lot of other people are in the same boat, right? That's why you're having the community dinner."

"Exactly. But a lot of people do attend with their family or friends. They enjoy having someone else make most of the meal." Jessica laughed. "And do the dishes. The inn has an industrial dishwasher."

"I can do without dishes and so can Herb," Mary said. "Count us in to volunteer and to eat. We bring something that day to share, right?"

"Yes we do," Jessica said. "The item depends on your last name. Both of you are 'B,' so you should bring dessert. I'm 'R,' so I'm doing a side dish."

Kaylee picked up a mini pumpkin. "If these don't sell, I see a lot of pies in my future." The others laughed.

"Actually, that brings me to another thing," Jessica said. "To raise money for the dinner, the Main Street businesses are going to hold a bake sale. We're calling it Anything But Pie. The rule is, you have to use pumpkin but you can't—"

"Make pie," Kaylee and Mary said in unison.

"Cute idea," Kaylee added. "It will be interesting to see how creative we can all get."

"That's what I thought." Jessica glanced at the wall clock and yelped. "I'd better get back. One of my employees is going off shift. See you later." With a jingle of bells, she dashed out the door.

The shop seemed quiet without their energetic friend. Kaylee reached under the counter and switched on the sound system. Soft music filled the air. "What's on the agenda today?"

Mary peered over her glasses at a note, then handed it to Kaylee. "Since we are going ahead with the specialty pumpkins, here's an order for what I think we'll need. Would you mind driving out to Madrona Grove Farm and Orchard to pick it up while I work on arrangements? That's where I got all these yesterday. It's a really nice drive."

At the word *drive*, Bear leaped up and began to cavort around Kaylee's stool, his nails skittering on the polished wood floor. They both smiled at his excitement.

"Looks like Bear wants to go." Kaylee finished her coffee. "And I love exploring the island, so the answer is yes."

"Great," Mary said. "I'll call ahead, and hopefully they'll have it ready for you when you get there."

Kaylee hopped into her red Ford Escape with Bear and set off toward the farm. Orcas Island was shaped like saddlebags, with the bay of East Sound dividing two land masses. Turtle Cove was in the western land mass and her destination in the eastern one, which meant she had to drive up one side of the fjord-like bay and down the other.

Her route cut through the inland countryside, a mix of forests and fields with occasional houses set among gardens or in the woods. The autumn peak had passed, but some orange and yellow leaves still clung and the hayfields were golden umber. November was usually the wettest month, but the good weather had held this year. Today the air was almost totally still, giving the landscape a placid peace as it basked in the sunshine.

"We'd better enjoy it while we can," Kaylee said to Bear. "Winter will be upon us soon enough."

They soon reached Eastsound, the largest town on the island. The medical center, library, and historical museum were here, along with a variety of other businesses. Kaylee detoured down Main Street, enjoying a glimpse of the charming and eclectic boutiques, shops, and eateries. As a shop owner now, she took a special interest in seeing how other business owners did window displays or otherwise made their stores inviting.

Kaylee thought back to her former employment as a professor of plant taxonomy at the University of Washington in Seattle, a position she'd suddenly lost due to department reorganization. Her grandmother, Bea Lyons, offered her a chance to transition from the ivory tower to retail, a move that required connecting with the community and her customers. Now she could apply the theoretical to real life.

After leaving the village behind, Kaylee took the road leading down the shore. The winding road offered water views on one side and verdant hills on the other. Now that summer was over, there were few sailboats in the water, but she spotted several fishermen in small boats and a fishing charter headed out to deeper water. This was salmon season after all.

At the end of the peninsula, she slowed, looking for Madrona

Grove Road. *There it is.* She signaled and turned, then immediately slowed. The road was no more than a lane, barely wide enough for two cars to pass. Dense shrubbery or brick walls hid large houses with waterfront property.

Past the last mansion, the road became dirt. Shrubby woods pressed close for a while, and then she saw a painted sign for the farm at the foot of a gravel driveway. A short way in, the woods vanished, giving way to fields on both sides. A white two-story frame farmhouse sat next to a charming brown barn surrounded by flower gardens and potted shrubs and trees. A few black-and-white hens pecked in the grass, free-range.

Bear sat up and stared at the birds, his ears at attention. "No, Bear. We're not chasing the chickens." She pulled the SUV into a space between a Volkswagen Beetle and a tan sedan. She fished for a leash and attached it to the excited little dog before exiting the car. Terrorized chickens would not get the relationship with the farm off on the right foot.

A middle-aged woman in faded jeans and a barn jacket was arranging a display of perennials in pots. She flicked her long, dark braid behind her shoulder and smiled at Kaylee, blue eyes crinkling. "Good morning. Can I help you?"

"Hi, I'm Kaylee Bleu from The Flower Patch over in Turtle Cove. I'm here to pick up an order of pumpkins."

The woman nodded and pointed to the open barn doors. "You'll want to talk to my husband, Paul. He's inside. I'm Violet Moore. Welcome to the farm."

"Nice to meet you," Kaylee said. She tugged at her dog's leash, trying to prevent him from lurching toward the farm owner. "Come on, Bear."

"What a cutie." Violet hunkered down and gave Bear a pat on the head. With a wag of his tail, he nuzzled her hand. "He's a lover."

"He sure is." Her appreciation of Bear warmed Kaylee's

heart. "We'll let you get back to work." Kaylee entered the barn, practically dragging Bear away from his new friend.

The interior was rustic, with that distinctive aroma of old wood and hay common to old barns. Tables and bins held an array of pumpkins, apples, and a selection of late vegetables. A man was loading a bin with huge bundles of leafy greens. Everything about him was nut-brown—his curly hair, tanned skin, and clothing. He glanced at Kaylee with narrow hazel eyes and nodded a greeting.

"What are those?" Kaylee asked, although it was not what she had planned to say.

"Collard greens." His hands continued to move as he stacked the bundles. "Fantastic with black-eyed peas and cornbread."

"Did someone say collards?" A woman darted out around a set of shelves holding dried herbs, sunflower seeds in packets, and jam. "Boyd, we have to get some. As my aunt in Georgia says, I love me some collards."

Surprised recognition jolted Kaylee. "Kathy? I didn't expect to see you here." Kathy Fitz was the head librarian at Orcas Island Library in Eastsound.

The librarian rocked back on her heels. "Kaylee, what are you doing here?" A handsome Native American man loomed up behind her, shaking his long, black hair into place. Kaylee wondered if he shared her Quinault ancestry, which she'd inherited from her father.

"I'm buying pumpkins for the shop. I could ask you the same thing." Kaylee smiled but she allowed her gaze to go beyond Kathy and rest on her companion. Bear investigated both newcomers with a thorough shoe sniffing.

"Doing a little shopping too. Kaylee Bleu, meet Boyd Parsons." Kathy tugged on the man's arm, bringing him forward. She looked up at him, her expression dreamy. "He's my ex-husband."

Kaylee quickly suppressed her shock. According to the story she'd heard, Kathy had gotten divorced twenty years ago from a man who cheated on her and had been happily single ever since.

"Nice to meet you, Boyd," she said, dimly aware that Paul had finished stacking the collards and left the barn. Hopefully he'd be back soon so she could ask about her order.

Boyd smiled at Kaylee but before he could speak, Kathy continued. "Boyd is a best-selling true crime writer. Maybe you've heard of him." She smiled proudly. "He's here working on an Orcas Island cold case for his next book."

"Of course I've heard of you." Kaylee realized she had seen Boyd's books, but she'd never connected him to Kathy. "Tell me more about your new project." Her pulse jumped in excitement. Due to her forensic botany work and the mysteries she'd solved in the past, she was eager to learn more.

Paul hadn't returned to the barn, but other customers were milling around the shop, including a mother and her toddler, as well as two men wearing windbreakers and khakis with binoculars around their necks. Orcas Island was popular with bird-watchers all year round.

Boyd chuckled, a deep rich sound. "Well, we know who the perpetrators were. It's the spoils of their crime I'm trying to find." He had the smooth, cultured voice of a classical music radio show host. "In the 1930s, a Seattle bank was robbed and one of the perpetrators, Lester Clayton, escaped to this island. He holed up with a widow who lived at Buttercup Cottage."

"That's right next door to this farm," Kathy added. "Boyd bought the place for a writing retreat."

"Killed two birds," Boyd said, not noticing the bird-watchers within earshot. "There's long been speculation about what happened to the proceeds of the robbery, as well as about Edna Taylor, the widow. Some wonder if she was in cahoots with Lester."

"People have searched for the loot over the years with no luck," Kathy put in. "But Boyd thinks he can figure it out."

Boyd's smile was modest. "I hope so. The other robbers claimed Lester was the bagman, so there's a good chance it's still here on the island."

"I assume Lester didn't say where he hid it." Kaylee pictured the man biding his time in jail until he could retrieve his ill-gotten fortune.

The writer sighed and shook his head. "Unfortunately, Lester was killed in a shoot-out at the cottage. And Edna claimed she had no knowledge of the money, never even saw it. She passed away from influenza soon after the event."

"It all sounds very intriguing," Kaylee said. "I can't wait to hear what you find out." Aware of time passing, she craned her neck looking for Paul. He was standing with Violet out by the perennials, speaking in low, intense tones. Then Paul pivoted and stalked back toward the barn. That was her cue. "It was great seeing you two, but I'd better grab my pumpkins and get going."

"We'll see you later, Kaylee. Have a good day." Kathy linked arms with Boyd and led him toward the collards. "I can't wait to cook you my special Southern good-luck meal."

"I can use plenty of that," Boyd said, giving that attractive chuckle again.

With a headshake of bemusement at the couple, who seemed on the best of terms despite their history, Kaylee hurried to intercept Paul. "I'm here to pick up an order of pumpkins for The Flower Patch."

He took the paper Kaylee handed to him and scanned it. "I have it ready for you. Bring your car around back and we'll load up."

Kaylee drove to the loading area and Paul helped her stow several crates of pumpkins in the rear. "If you need more, let me know," the farmer said. "We've got plenty." His lips curved in a brief smile. "Though they are going fast."

"I'll bet," Kaylee said. "According to my designer, they're really hot this year."

Paul scratched his curly head. "Violet told me ornamentals would extend the season past Halloween and she was right. Never thought I'd see the day pumpkins would be described as fashionable. Wonders never cease."

"That's for sure." With a laugh, Kaylee thanked him and hopped back into her car. As she drove slowly along the rutted lane leading back to the drive, she saw the two bird-watchers again. The short, stout one waved at her to stop. Thinking they needed directions or perhaps bird information, she braked and rolled down her window.

They trotted up to the car. The stout one leaned in her window. "Hey, miss. You're from around here, right?" At her nod, he asked, "Do you really think there's buried treasure on this island? Or is that guy just trying to sell books?"

"I honestly have no idea," Kaylee said. "I'm fairly new to Orcas." With a wave, she pressed the gas again. She couldn't blame the men for asking. The idea of finding a bank robber's hidden spoils was enticing.

2

"Tonight I brought something a little extra." Mary set a thermos of hot cider on the table in the meeting room. "Besides this." The Petal Pushers garden club met on Tuesdays in the public room of the Old Cape Lighthouse's keeper's cottage, a historic building with a water view. Mary foraged in a second large tote bag and pulled out four orange pumpkins about the size of cantaloupes.

"Halloween's been over for a while," DeeDee Wilcox said dubiously. DeeDee owned Between the Lines, a mystery bookstore near The Flower Patch. In addition to selling books, she made wonderful handmade goat milk soap and skin care products, which she sold at Kaylee's shop.

"I realize that," Mary said. "We're making table ornaments for Thanksgiving." Next out of her bag was a selection of hand tools and a drill.

"If Mary gets her way, we'll be selling pumpkins until Christmas." Kaylee grabbed a dark chocolate brownie from the plate Jessica had contributed from her bakery. Sitting at her feet, Bear begged with a whine. "No chocolate for you, Bear." She tossed him a dog treat instead, then took a bite of her brownie. "Yum, cream cheese. These are awesome, Jess."

"Thank you kindly. New recipe." Jessica took it upon herself to pour the cider since Mary was busy. "That looks dangerous," she said, waving at the drill. "Are you sure you trust us with that thing?"

"I'll do the drilling," Mary said. "I only have one drill anyway. But you can create the designs." The last thing out of her bag was

15

an example for them to reference—a pumpkin decorated with small drilled starbursts and lit by a battery-powered votive. Unlike a jack-o'-lantern, which usually had the top cut open, the bottom of this pumpkin had been removed to accommodate the light.

"Oh, a little lantern!" DeeDee said, clasping her hands together. "I love it. The girls will too, especially Zoe." Zoe was her eleven-year-old daughter, sister to the eight-year-old Polly. "I might make heart shapes on mine. They'll flip over that."

"We should do some for the community Thanksgiving dinner," Kaylee suggested. "They'd be great centerpieces."

"Good idea," Jessica said. "Let's add it to the plan. We can get other volunteers to help." She dispensed refills of cider, the brownies went around again, and the women began creating their designs, working on paper first.

"I had an interesting encounter at Madrona Grove Farm today," Kaylee said. "I ran into Kathy Fitz and her ex-husband."

DeeDee whistled. "Boyd Parsons? Is he still a hunk? He looks like it in his author photos, but those glamour shots are often deceptive."

Jessica narrowed her eyes. "You mean is he still a no-good cheating rat? He broke Kathy's heart, as I recall. It was pretty ugly. She was depressed for a long time."

Kaylee put up a hand. "I have no idea about the rat part. He *is* gorgeous and well-spoken. The two of them seemed happy together."

"Oh, don't tell me that." Jessica put a hand to her forehead in a dramatic gesture. "Oliver lost a whole flower today and now I know why." Oliver was her lavender geranium, credited for revealing omens of bad events to come. "I can't believe Kathy would even consider reconciling with that man. He's going to break her heart again."

Mary was busy cutting the bottoms off the pumpkins, then

scooping out seeds and insides onto a newspaper. "That's not fair, Jess. He might have changed, seen the error of his ways. It can happen."

"I hope so," Jessica muttered. "Or else he'd better watch out." She stabbed her pencil onto her paper extra hard as though to emphasize her wrath.

"I'll warn him you're armed with that pencil," DeeDee said dryly. "Speaking of exes, Violet Moore, who owns Madrona Grove Farm, used to date Boyd. That was a few years after he and Kathy split up."

Kaylee thought of the tense conversation she'd witnessed between husband and wife. Had they been arguing about Boyd? "I met her today. She and her husband both seem nice."

"They are," Mary said. "I like to shop there. Support your local farmers, you know."

"If you lined up Boyd's exes, they'd make a bridge to the mainland," Jessica said.

DeeDee sent her a look. "I will say, as far as *writing* goes," she said, "Boyd is excellent. His breakout book resulted in an innocent man being released from jail."

"I think I read that one," Mary said. "It was about a casino robbery in Nevada, right?"

The bookstore owner nodded. "One of the employees was killed during a hostage situation and a guy named Eldon Landis was arrested. Boyd did some sleuthing and found out Eldon had been framed. They arrested the real killer and set Eldon free. Not that Eldon was a choirboy by any means, but he wasn't in on that robbery."

"It *was* a good book," Jessica said grudgingly. "I'll give him that. Luke loved it." Luke was Jessica's husband, a tax accountant. "He especially liked reading about how casinos manage their money."

"Boyd was on all the talk shows back then." DeeDee picked up her cup of cider, her expression thoughtful. "I wonder if I can book him for an author talk."

"Probably," Kaylee said. She was drawing flowers for her pumpkin design. "He just bought a house on the island. Buttercup Cottage." She watched the effect of this bombshell on her friends.

Jessica slapped the table. "Boyd bought a house here? Nothing good will come of that. Poor Kathy."

Mary raised her eyebrows. "Buttercup Cottage? Why, that's where a bank robber hid out during the Depression."

DeeDee's mind was on her shop. "He's moving to the island? Then I'll definitely be able to book him." She tilted her head. "If I do it soon, I can really boost Christmas sales."

Kaylee smiled. "Hold that thought, DeeDee. Jess, we'll talk to Kathy and be there for her, no matter what. And Mary, as a matter of fact, Boyd's next book is based entirely on Lester Clayton and the bank robbery."

"A Boyd Parsons book set on Orcas Island?" DeeDee asked with a rapturous expression. "Now I know I've died and gone to heaven." She grabbed a brownie and took a big bite.

"But wait. There's more." Kaylee put up a hand with a smile. "Boyd thinks he can find the proceeds of the robbery. No one ever has, apparently."

"No, but they've dug holes all over the island looking for it." Mary handed out rolls of thin, black tape. "Put a strip around the middle of your pumpkin so your dots will be level."

The other women followed her example, then began to draw their designs on the hollowed-out pumpkins with markers.

"How's this?" Jessica handed Mary her pumpkin, banded with rows of dots in a sophisticated pattern. "Buried treasure, huh? Maybe we can get in on that." She sighed. "Wouldn't it be great to find it? I could pay off our house and help Mila with her student loans." Mila was Jessica and Luke's adult daughter.

"In that case, we'd have to see what the law says. The bank may still have a claim." Mary picked up the drill and switched it on. Startled, Bear darted to the far side of the room. After realizing it wasn't going to hurt him, he trotted back to Kaylee's side.

Mary deftly drilled holes in Jessica's pumpkin, then did the same to the others. Next, the battery lights were inserted and switched on, highlighting the creative patterns they'd made.

Kaylee admired the glowing flower cutouts adorning her orange pumpkin, thinking they were much nicer than a scary jack-o'-lantern. Who knew a pumpkin could be so pretty? "Let's do some of these for the shop."

Mary laughed. "I was hoping you'd say that. I think they'll be big sellers. And we can spray them with a bleach solution as a preservative."

"I'm going to take mine home and put it in the entryway as a night-light," Jessica said. She turned her pumpkin around, examining every side. "This was fun. But before we adjourn, I did want to discuss the bake sale next week. As I may have mentioned, we can make whatever we want as long as it contains pumpkin and isn't pie."

"I'll make my pumpkin scones and whoopie pies," Mary said. "Those are always a hit."

"I'll have to think about what I'll make," DeeDee said. "Maybe I'll do cookies. How does pumpkin chocolate chip sound? The girls can help me. They love making cookies." She smiled. "And eating the dough."

"Don't let them eat too much. I'd like you to bring six dozen cookies." Jessica wrote a note on her pad. "I'm making pumpkin truffles and pumpkin chocolate cupcakes from original recipes. Mine have to include chocolate, of course, because people expect that from me." She looked at Kaylee in inquiry. "Any thoughts?"

"Um, no. Not yet," Kaylee hedged. She wasn't as experienced a baker as the others. "Let me do some research and I'll get back to you soon, I promise."

"By the end of the week, okay?" Jessica put her notepad away. "I want to make a flyer and place ads in the paper so people will get excited about the bake sale."

Oh boy. Her name publicly associated with a baked item? Kaylee resolved to find something stunning but not too hard. That might be a challenge.

The meeting broke up soon after, and Kaylee and Bear headed home to Wildflower Cottage, located a couple of miles from downtown. As a child, she'd enjoyed staying with her grandparents in the cozy, white farmhouse surrounded by fields of lavender. Living there was one of the best things about her new life, and every time she arrived home, a deep peace swept over her. Even now in late fall, she could smell the aroma of *Lavandula* drifting from the dormant fields.

Inside, she gave Bear a fresh bowl of water and an evening snack, then went to the master bedroom to get ready for bed. She was washing her face when her cell phone buzzed on the nightstand.

The screen flashed the caller's name: *Grandma.* Kaylee's heart skipped a beat. Why was Bea calling so late? Scenarios of illness or broken bones flashed through her mind. "Hello?" She could hear the fear in her voice and she cleared her throat. "Grandma?" There, that was better.

"Hello, Kaylee." Bea's voice was full of warmth and life. "Did I scare you, calling so late? I'm sorry. I guessed you probably just got home from the Petal Pushers meeting." Bea had been a member before she moved away.

Kaylee plopped down on the bed, relief coursing through her. "You did surprise me a little. I just got home about five minutes ago."

"How was the meeting?" Bea sighed. "I miss them."

Come visit. "Tonight, Jess was roping us all into this Anything But Pie bake sale to benefit the community Thanksgiving dinner. Oh, and we drilled holes in pumpkins. Rather, Mary did." Kaylee kicked off her shoes and wiggled her toes. Bear, finished with his snack, trotted into the room and jumped up on the bed to snuggle.

"Holes in pumpkins? That's quite the thing now. I saw that in a home and garden magazine. Really nice for decorations."

Kaylee ran her hand along Bear's silky fur. "I agree. Mary sent me to Madrona Grove Farm today to buy tons of those tiny ornamental pumpkins. We're making arrangements and decorations for Thanksgiving and maybe even Christmas." Kaylee went on with details, knowing that her florist grandmother liked to talk shop.

"Send me pictures," Bea said. "Your plans sound lovely."

Kaylee opened her mouth to say something, thought better of it, then went ahead. "I wish you were going to be here with me for Thanksgiving. Is there any way . . .?"

Bea sighed. "I'm afraid not, honey. It costs so much to fly around the holidays. And it's so crowded and crazy. How about I come for Easter?"

That was almost six months away. "All right. I'll take what I can get." Kaylee knew she sounded grumpy but didn't try too hard to perk up her attitude. What good was having a grandmother if you couldn't be yourself, even if a bit childish and graceless at times? At her tone, Bear picked up his head, his ears pricked. "It's okay, Bear," she whispered. "I'm just disappointed."

"Oh, by the way." Bea changed the subject. "I heard that Boyd Parsons is writing a book about Edna Taylor and the bank robber."

"What?" Kaylee rocked back against her pillows, swinging her legs up onto the bed. "How did you hear that? I only found out about it today."

Bea's tone was smug. "I still have connections on the island, my dear. And news that juicy can't be contained." She chuckled. "And Kathy Fitz needs to have her head examined, bless her heart. Boyd's charming and interesting, but he's not reliable in the least. As they say, once a . . . well, you know." She didn't need to finish.

"You really are tied into the gossip network," Kaylee said in admiration. "Maybe I should call you for news."

"Maybe so. Anyway, I have something to tell you about Edna. Back in the 1930s, The Flower Patch building was home to several small businesses. She ran her seamstress business out of there."

"I didn't know that," Kaylee said. She pictured a sewing shop, with bolts of cloth and dressmaker dummies. Maybe it had been in The Flower Patch's main room.

"She stitched curtains and upholstery as well as clothing," Bea said. "When I bought the building, I found several boxes and trunks in the attic that belonged to her."

That piece of information startled Kaylee out of her relaxed state. She sat bolt upright, ignoring Bear, who grumbled at being disturbed. "Do you think there is anything in there related to the bank robbery?" Bear sighed and curled up again.

"I don't know. I remember seeing a lot of papers and some cloth and notions. Nothing too interesting, but I never disposed of it all either. I always had in the back of my mind that I'd go through it more carefully in case there was something of historic value."

"Why did the robber pick Edna's place to hide in, do you know?" That part had bothered Kaylee since she heard the story. How terrible it would be to have a fugitive criminal barge into your home.

Bea snorted softly. "That was never really determined. Some said he landed his boat nearby and hers was the first house he found. Others thought she knew him from the past and he sought her out specifically."

"What do you think?"

"I'm not sure," Bea said. "From what I know of Edna, she was a respectable, churchgoing woman. It doesn't seem likely she would willingly be involved with or aid a bank robber." She paused. "Maybe you'll find the answer in her things."

They disconnected a few minutes later, with Kaylee promising to keep Bea updated regarding the mystery around Edna Taylor. She finished getting ready for bed, grateful to crawl between the soft flannel sheets, but somehow sleep eluded her. She imagined the robber pulling his boat up in Madrona Grove in the dead of night. Then he would steal through the woods and fields, seeking shelter. Why Orcas Island? There were 172 islands in the San Juan chain—only a handful were occupied, true, but there were many places a man could hide. Almost 100 years before, even fewer people had lived on these islands. They were isolated, undeveloped, and pristine.

Lester had seen the cottage lights. Then what greeted him? A joyous welcome or frightened screaming? Kaylee had trouble deciding.

She needed to see their faces. Sitting up and switching on the lamp to Bear's disgruntlement, Kaylee picked up her phone. She opened a browser and searched for Lester Clayton. To her surprise, he was movie-star handsome, with a square jaw and straight brows over intense light-colored eyes. He had been only twenty-six when he died.

Edna Taylor was younger than Kaylee had expected, with abundant dark hair, defined cheekbones, and dark lipstick on her full lips—or at least it appeared so in the black-and-white photo. She was twenty-four when she passed away from the flu. According to the information online, she'd been a teenage bride and then widowed when her husband was killed in an accident.

Kaylee set her phone back on the nightstand. Now she had images to go with the names, but her research had been inconclusive. Had the young seamstress been a victim or an accomplice?

She could hardly wait to find out.

3

At a knock on her front door early the next morning, Kaylee got up from the kitchen table, where she'd been enjoying coffee and poached eggs, and let in her guest. It was Reese Holt, and, as always, her heart lifted when she saw the tall, muscular handyman with his sandy brown hair and blue eyes. They'd become friends since she'd moved to Turtle Cove and she enjoyed his company. "Morning, Reese. What brings you out here?"

"I'm doing a tune-up on the furnace today." Setting down his toolbox, Reese crouched and patted Bear, who was whining and wagging his tail in excitement. He grinned. "Did you forget?"

Apparently she had, although she usually remembered everything to do with Reese. Bea had always hired him when the cottage needed maintenance or repairs, and Kaylee had continued the arrangement. "Come on in. Want a cup of coffee?"

"Sure." Reese spotted her decorated pumpkin, sitting on the counter next to a pile of mail. "That's creative. I like it."

"It's something new we're doing at the shop." Kaylee filled a mug with steaming coffee and doctored it the way Reese liked it—a splash of milk, no sugar. "Mary's idea."

Reese was still examining the pumpkin. "You used a drill to make those holes, right? Thanks." He took the mug and sipped. "Good coffee."

Kaylee sat at the table and picked up her fork. "Mary did the drilling. It was safer that way."

Reese gave a bark of laughter and pulled out a chair. As he

settled his lanky limbs at the table, Kaylee noticed how well the faded greens and blues of the flannel he wore over his T-shirt suited his coloring.

They sat in companionable silence for a few minutes, Reese continuing to give Bear his due while Kaylee finished her breakfast. She carried the empty plate to the sink, then brought the coffee carafe over for refills.

"What else needs to be done here today?" Kaylee asked. She liked having someone keep an eye on her home and shop and perform scheduled maintenance. It was one responsibility she didn't have to fret about. Going from living in a tiny apartment to owning two historic buildings was quite a leap.

Reese pulled out a small notebook and opened it. "After I check the furnace, I'll go up on the roof and make sure the shingles and flashing are good and tight. Then I'll go around and check the windows and doors, and the basement too. I want to make sure everything seals properly. You'll appreciate that when it snows."

"Thank you." Kaylee gazed out the window at the overcast sky. "I can't believe winter is almost upon us."

"Me neither. Summer is never, ever long enough, especially way up here next to Canada." He sipped his coffee. "Think you'll take the boat out again, or should we winterize that too?"

Her grandfather's boat, the *KayBea*. Kaylee often got so busy she forgot the pleasure she found in taking the center console launch for a cruise.

"Let's not winterize it yet. I want to go out one more time this year." She glanced outside again at the thickening clouds. "The next nice day." She smiled at Reese. "What would you say to coming with me? I'll bring a picnic. If you can spare the time, that is." Reese's handyman services were in high demand on the island.

"I'm never too busy for a cruise in the *KayBea*," he said

lightly, pushing back his chair. "Let me know when and I'll be there." He stood and ferried his cup to the sink. "I'd better get to work." He winked. "Duty calls."

Kaylee noticed the time and yelped. "And I should run. See you later, Reese."

He lugged his toolbox down to the basement and Kaylee finished getting ready to the sound of pipes clanking and banging. She hadn't had a chance to tell him about Boyd's investigation into the 1930s bank robbery and the possibility that The Flower Patch attic held clues. Reese enjoyed history so he'd like hearing about the revival of the cold case. But no doubt she'd have another opportunity to talk to him about it soon.

Reese was a fixture in her life, she realized, and she liked that very much.

All the way to the flower shop, she thought about an excursion in the *KayBea*. With so many tiny, uninhabited islands in the San Juans, there were endless opportunities to explore. Some isles were home to seabirds, while others featured gorgeous wildflowers in spring.

Mary was already working when Kaylee arrived. She glanced up with a smile. "Oh, I love Bear's bow tie. It's such fun seeing what you put on him every day." Bear cocked his head, seeming to preen as Mary admired the tie, which featured tiny dogs surrounded by autumn leaves.

"It's fun finding them," Kaylee admitted, shrugging out of her jacket. "Choosing them is like making a statement about the time of year, the weather, even my mood. And Bear's of course." He yipped in agreement.

"That one is perfect for a fall day." Mary slid a tall disposable cup toward Kaylee. "I bought us provisions at Death by Chocolate. We have a lot of work to do." She gestured to the windows, now dressed with the pumpkin creations Mary had put together. "We have a rush order from the Tortoiseshell Hotel for dining room centerpieces and lobby displays."

"That's fantastic. I've been hoping to get their business more often." The Tortoiseshell Hotel was one of the nicest lodging establishments on the island. Their orders were both lucrative and flattering, a testament to the quality of The Flower Patch's work and reputation. Kaylee picked up the cup and sipped. "Yum. What's in this?"

"It's cinnamon spice coffee with real cream." Mary smiled. "This time of year is a perfect excuse to indulge." She opened a white paper bag. "I also bought a couple of muffins." The big pumpkin muffins were studded with chocolate chips.

Despite not being the least bit hungry after eating eggs for breakfast, Kaylee took a bite anyway. The soft, lightly spiced muffin melted in her mouth, releasing bursts of chocolate flavor. "Oh my. I can feel the sugar working already. Point me in the right direction."

Mary consulted the order form. "First we need two of those cranberry-colored pottery urns from the back room."

Kaylee set down her snack and lugged the two containers into the work area. There she helped Mary create a stunning whimsical arrangement of *Helianthus annuus*—red and yellow sunflowers—with miniature white and orange pumpkins. They also added seeded eucalyptus, a combination of pale green seedpods and leaves that contrasted nicely with the other shapes and colors.

"They are going to love these. They're like something out of a fairy tale," Kaylee said. She moved the urns to one side for delivery later that day. "What are we doing for the centerpieces?"

Mary pulled out a box and opened the flaps. "I was thinking these would be good for the bases." She set a circular piece cut from a log on the worktable. "We can do white pumpkins and bittersweet vine." She pulled out a short candle glass. "And one of these in the middle."

"Love it." Kaylee began to sort through the bins of pumpkins to find white ones around the right size.

"We'll have to gather the pieces, then assemble them on-site," Mary said. "We need two dozen."

"I'll go," Kaylee volunteered. "Show me what you're thinking first and then I'll pack the car."

Together they decided on a simple but attractive display and then carefully packed boxes with the goods. "I'll run out there now in the shop van," Kaylee said. "Then on the way back, I'm going to swing by the library, if that's okay with you. It will be lunchtime anyway." She wanted to check out cookbooks for bake sale ideas. Although Kaylee enjoyed browsing recipes online, it was nowhere near as relaxing as leafing through actual cookbooks, especially vintage ones. She'd gotten into the habit while learning to cook and bake with Bea.

"You're the boss," Mary said brightly. "I brought leftover pea soup. If you don't get a chance to grab something, you can eat when you get back."

Kaylee picked up a carton. "That sounds perfect. I love your pea soup." Having Mary in her life was almost like having Bea around. They were both caring and practical, and great cooks besides. She was a lucky woman. "I'll have to leave Bear here. Neither the library nor the inn would welcome him, I'm afraid."

Mary reached out and patted the little dog, who had been watching them work. "That's never a problem, you know that." She whispered to Bear, "I know where the treats are kept." He wagged his tail and gave a little yip.

"I'll see you two later then. Thanks, Mary." Arms full, Kaylee backed through the shop door.

The Tortoiseshell Hotel was on the road to Eastsound, only

a mile or two out of town. The sprawling white building with its long porch was both elegant and welcoming. The venue hosted many upscale weddings, parties, and other events, and Kaylee appreciated being on their recommended list.

Inside the spacious lobby, Kaylee asked for Charlie Moore, the manager. The desk clerk picked up a phone and a minute later, Charlie came bustling from the direction of the dining room. "Good morning, Kaylee," she said. "Thanks for bringing those over so quickly."

As Kaylee greeted the manager, she realized that she resembled someone—Paul Moore. Charlie, whose given name was Charlotte, had the same curly, brown hair and tanned complexion as Paul, who must be her brother or cousin.

After lugging in the boxes with the help of the clerk, she asked, "Are you related to Paul Moore? We bought these pumpkins at his farm."

Charlie laughed as she touched one of the white pumpkins with a delicate finger. "Isn't that a coincidence? Yes, he's my brother. I'm glad we're supporting him, even if it's indirectly. He's worked so hard to make a go of that farm."

Kaylee spent the next hour setting up the centerpieces and arranging the lobby urns. After the manager presented her with a check for payment and gushed over her work, she headed to the library.

Orcas Island Library was a small, gray building tucked just off Main Street. She pulled into an empty space in the parking lot and went in.

Kaylee loved libraries and had spent many happy hours in them. And as a college student and professor, they had been her lifeline to the information and research she needed. As the familiar scent of leather, wood, paper, and ink embraced her, she took a deep breath. The entrance led directly into the main room, where the front desk was placed. Behind the desk were lines of bookcases and a row of public computers. To the left and right were the children's room and the reading room.

"Hello, Kaylee." With a smile, Kathy Fitz greeted her from behind the desk. Today her glossy hair was pulled up into a bun, with a few artful curls hanging at her ears. She wore a cerulean silk blouse with a black pencil skirt—the very picture of attractive efficiency.

"Hi Kathy. I'm here to look at cookbooks." Kaylee glanced around and spotted Boyd's dark head at one of the computer terminals. No doubt he was doing research for his book—or maybe just checking e-mails. Perhaps Buttercup Cottage didn't have Internet access.

"Any type of food in particular?" Kathy asked.

"Cookies, pastries, candy—anything pumpkin but pie." Kaylee laughed. "It's for our bake sale next week."

Kathy came around the end of the desk. "Oh yes, I heard about that. I think we have several that will be useful." She led the way to the reference department, where cookbooks of many cuisines were lined along the shelf. She ran her finger along the titles and pulled out three, handing them to Kaylee. "Why don't you go through these? If you find something you like, you can check out that book."

"Sounds like a plan," Kaylee said. She carried the books to the closest table and sat down. She opened the first and began to leaf through, enjoying the photographs of luscious baked goods. While she was browsing, Boyd got up and left the computer station. He went to the desk and spoke to Kathy in low tones.

She ought to tell him about Edna's belongings in The Flower Patch attic. She pushed back from the table then hesitated. Maybe she should wait until she'd had a chance to look through them. It would be a shame to get his hopes up only to find a bunch of old patterns and pins.

Boyd left the library after a few more minutes of chatting with Kathy. Shortly after that, Kaylee brought the books up to the desk. "I'll take this one," she said, choosing a volume that contained a recipe for pumpkin macarons. Those would attract attention for sure—if she pulled them off. But how hard could they be? She was a scientist after all, and she remembered making them with Bea when she was a teen.

"Good choice," Kathy said. It was her standard response to the books her patrons signed out. She scanned the book, then placed it on the counter and whispered, "Guess what? Boyd thinks he knows where the missing fortune is."

4

Kaylee's pulse leaped. "He figured it out already?" She leaned forward and lowered her voice too. "Can you tell me about it?"

Kathy grinned. "He found information that leads him to believe that Lester's first stop was Blossom Island. It's one of those uninhabited islands, but there was a cabin built when someone squatted there back in the 1920s. He wants to go out there and look. But first he needs to find a boat."

Before Kaylee could think about it, she blurted, "I have a boat he can use."

"Really? Are you sure? He doesn't have a license."

"No problem. I'll pilot."

"That's super! Thank you." Kathy's eyes sparkled with excitement. "I know he wants to get out there within the next few days, before the weather gets bad."

Someone pushed past Kaylee and plunked a stack of books on the counter. "I'd like to check out, please." Violet Moore, the farmer's wife, glared at Kathy.

"Of course," Kathy said, taking Violet's card. "Kaylee is all set." She swiped the card and watched to make sure the computer opened the account.

Kaylee edged aside, studying Violet with curiosity as she continued to glower at the librarian. "We love the pumpkins you sold us," Kaylee said, trying to lighten the woman's mood. "And so do our customers. Earlier today, I brought some centerpieces and arrangements to the Tortoiseshell Hotel."

"That's good." Violet tossed the words over her shoulder.

"Listen, Kathy. I know I can't tell you what to do, but you should be careful."

Kathy's brows shot up. "What do you mean?" She picked up one of Violet's books and held it toward the scanner.

Violet glanced around, then lowered her voice. Apparently she didn't mind if Kaylee overheard. "Boyd. You know he's not trustworthy."

Giving a brittle laugh, Kathy shook her head. "What do you care, Violet? You're happily married to Paul." She checked out the next book and placed it on top of the first, then picked up a third.

The farmer's wife shifted from one foot to the other. "That's true. But it doesn't mean I can't warn others to stay away from Boyd." She snorted. "He really raked me over the coals. It took me a year to get over him."

Kathy's cheeks reddened and a fierce light shone in her brown eyes. "Boyd has changed. Not that it's any of your business, but he asked for my forgiveness." She stood straight, her shoulders back. "In my opinion, that's a sign of sincerity. And maturity."

Violet grabbed her stack of books and stuffed them into a cloth bag. "Or it's a sign he's fattening you up for the kill," she muttered.

"What was that?" Kathy's tone was sharp. She crossed her arms. "Have a good day, Violet. Oh, and tell Paul we enjoyed the squash and potatoes very much."

With a grunt, Violet clutched her bag of books and marched toward the front door. She pushed through, letting the door swing shut behind her.

"I guess I'll get going," Kaylee said. "Mary is expecting me back at the shop."

Kathy was still staring after Violet, her expression thoughtful. She shook herself and blinked. "What? Oh yes, don't let me keep you. I'll call you later about the boat, if that's okay."

"I think it sounds fun." Kaylee decided to go ahead and mention Edna's belongings. "Tell Boyd I may have some of Edna's things in my shop attic. I haven't looked at them yet, though, so I don't know how useful they'll be."

Now Kaylee had the librarian's full attention. "That's awesome. I'll be sure to mention it to him." Kathy practically bounced with glee. "This whole thing is so exciting. I feel like I'm on one of those investigative television shows."

"Me too," Kaylee said. "I hope we find the treasure." She was tempted to be a little nosy and ask Kathy more about her relationship with Boyd, but she refrained. They weren't quite gossip-level friends. Besides, Kathy was a grown woman. Surely she could take care of herself.

Back at the shop, Mary greeted Kaylee with the news that she already had orders for pumpkin lanterns, centerpieces, and garlands. "At this rate, we'll need to get another order from the farm," Mary said.

Kaylee crouched down and said hello to Bear, who acted as if he hadn't seen her for weeks, judging by how he rolled around begging for a good tummy rub. "That's great news. I actually saw Violet at the library." She filled Mary in on the encounter.

Mary continued to put together a bouquet of fall flowers as they talked. "I do remember Violet dating Boyd. She was head over heels for him, but he took a newspaper job in Seattle and didn't take her with him. A couple of years later, she married Paul." Mary reached for her scissors to clip the stems and Kaylee handed them to her.

"She seemed pretty upset today," Kaylee said. "Maybe she

never got over him." It might seem counterintuitive, but she'd seen women warn others away from a man because they had feelings for him. Poor Paul, if so. Thinking of him reminded her of his sister. "By the way, Charlie Moore loved the pumpkins. I didn't know she and Paul were related, but now that I've met him, I see the resemblance."

Mary wrapped the bouquet in plastic and tissue and applied a sticker. "Charlie has had a bit of a hard time in years past, but she seems to have landed on her feet." She handed the bouquet to Kaylee. "Can you please put that in the cooler? The customer should be in pretty soon to pick it up."

As Kaylee opened the front cooler, a couple of men passing by on the sidewalk caught her eye. The way they had their faces practically pressed against the glass was difficult to ignore. She set the flowers on the cooler shelf and shut the door, then took a good look at them.

She recognized the two bird-watchers and gave them a friendly wave and a smile. In response, however, they only continued to stare, solemn-faced.

"Who's out there?" Mary asked. "Someone we know?"

"No, just a couple of men I've seen around. Tourists." Kaylee watched as they turned away from the shop and kept going. She thought she saw them go into Death by Chocolate. At least they'd be supporting Jessica with their dollars, if not The Flower Patch.

Kaylee returned to the counter. "What's next, Mary? Tell me what you need."

The rest of the afternoon flew by as the two florists waited on customers, took orders, and put together arrangements. Most of the patrons admired the pumpkin displays and several placed orders for Thanksgiving. As the pumpkins sold, Mary noted how many more they would need to get.

Around five, Mary left for the day and Kaylee prepared to

lock up. In her usual routine, she made a circuit upstairs to be sure everything was secure and in place. All she needed was an open window to send the heat bill soaring or let a deluge of rain into the building that could damage the floors or walls.

On the second floor, the office and workroom were in good order. Bear started to trundle back downstairs, but Kaylee hesitated, her eyes on the stairs to the third floor. She wasn't hungry yet thanks to Mary's hearty soup, and she still had a little energy. "Come on, Bear," she called. "We're going up to the attic." He scampered back up to join her.

Light from the open door below barely illuminated the dark space, but it was enough for Kaylee to find and pull on the string of a lone bulb. She hadn't been up here very often, and she was overwhelmed each time by the amount and variety of things crammed inside. She gazed around at the armoire against one wall, stacks of boxes, racks of covered clothing, and other intriguing items. Where to begin?

Kaylee pulled out her phone and dialed her grandmother. When Bea answered, she said, "I'm in the attic trying to find the stuff that belonged to Edna Taylor. Before I start excavating, can you give me a hint about where it might be?"

Her grandmother chuckled. "I hear you. That attic was almost full when I bought the place. Now it's ridiculous."

"Someday I'll get around to sorting through everything," Kaylee said.

"That's what I always said." Bea was silent for a moment. "Are you near the top of the stairs? Okay, go to the chimney to your left and look behind that, against the back wall. Edna's belongings include a green steamer trunk, a tall wooden trunk, and several wooden crates with lids." She chuckled again. "If I didn't know better, I'd think she had been packing to leave."

Perhaps she had been, with her paramour Lester Clayton. Kaylee took a few tentative steps toward the area. "It's so dark I'm going to need my phone. Hold on." She turned on the flashlight application to light the way, Bear snuffling at everything they passed.

Tucked behind the chimney was the green metal trunk. Kaylee crouched down, shoving a wooden ironing board out of the way. She shone the light on the luggage tag. *Edna Taylor*, it read, followed by the shop's Main Street address.

She put the phone to her ear. "I found it, Grandma. Thanks."

"Let me know what you dig up. You've gotten me all curious."

"I will." Kaylee flipped the trunk latch up. "Oh, another thing happened today. Kathy Fitz told me Boyd needs someone to take him to Blossom Island by boat. He found some evidence that Lester Clayton might have gone there before coming to Orcas. I volunteered to take him in the *KayBea*."

"Blossom Island, you said? Your grandfather and I took a ride out there once. Not much to see, although the flowers are pretty in the spring."

"Kathy said something similar. It will be a neat trip, no matter what we find." Kaylee and her grandmother chatted a few minutes more about the adventure. After she disconnected, she placed the phone so its light would shine into the trunk.

Holding her breath with anticipation, she flung the lid open. She'd always considered digging around in old boxes and trunks a form of detecting. Perhaps it was a holdover from the mysteries she'd read as a young girl, when fictional investigators found secret diaries or other valuables in dusty attics.

An odor of mothballs and dust drifted from the trunk. At her side, Bear sneezed. Kaylee reached into the chest and lifted out thick, green velvet fabric folded into a rectangle. Below it was another layer of the same fabric. Her spirits sinking, she unfolded the first bundle. The wide hem and rod pocket gave it away. The box was full of curtains. *Unsold merchandise from*

Edna's shop, maybe? She stuffed the first one back in and shut the lid.

Feeling silly over her disappointment that the first box hadn't yielded the treasure, she stood and lifted a wooden crate off a pile of three. Fortunately, the lid wasn't nailed on. Inside were sewing tools, notions, rolls of thread, and button cards, perfect for someone who collected vintage sewing supplies. Unfortunately, it wasn't much use to her at the moment.

Bear whined and thumped his tail against the floor, a sure sign he was getting restless and hungry for dinner. "Just a few more minutes, Bear, I promise." While she was here, she might as well be thorough and check all of Edna's luggage.

Next she opened the tall wooden chest, which was filled with clothing. Delicate, hand-stitched nightgowns, baby clothing, and a dozen or so dresses, all made with lovely fabric and worthy of further examination at some point. Maybe the historical museum would want some of the items for their exhibits.

A large crate held a black electric Singer sewing machine, with the company name printed in gold. It was a beauty, sleek and simple.

She hit pay dirt in the last crate, or at least the possibility. The crate held letters, ledgers, bank statements, photographs, and more, all thrown inside without regard to organization or order. It was the most likely place to find a tie between Edna and Lester.

After closing the box, Kaylee stood and stretched. The rain that had threatened all day drummed on the roof overhead. Taking another breath, she tested the weight of the crate. She'd lug the papers home and go through them in a spot with decent light. "All right, let's go eat," she told Bear. He jumped down from an old rocker, leaving it swaying, his collar tags jingling in eagerness.

In the parking lot, Kaylee opened the SUV's hatch and stowed the crate. She'd draped her raincoat over it in case the wooden slats leaked, so she and Bear got soaked on the short distance to the car from the shop. She scooped up the shivering dog and tucked him inside, then reached for the towel she kept handy to rub him off in such situations. She would have to wait to get dry until she got home, thankfully a short drive.

"What do you think, Bear? Fire tonight?" Kaylee started the engine and set the heat to the highest setting, even if it wouldn't kick in for a few minutes. Just the idea of hot air was comforting on a cold, wet night like this.

Kaylee checked her mirrors, then pulled out into the street without needing to wait for traffic. At this time of night during the off-season, everyone else was already home, sitting in front of their own fires. Tires splashing and windshield wipers flapping frantically, she navigated the familiar route.

She hadn't gone a block when a set of headlights appeared behind her. To her surprise they were approaching fast—too fast for the street's speed limit and the weather conditions. Kaylee bit her lip with annoyance and maintained her steady pace.

The headlights grew larger, slowing only when they reached her back bumper. The vehicle was larger than hers, a truck probably, so the lights shone right into her modest-size SUV. With a huff of irritation, she adjusted the rearview mirror. Then she squinted at the dark road ahead.

Away from town, the night was inky and the road narrow. With the rain driving down, she could barely see the painted lines. She slowed to a crawl.

The headlights inched even closer.

There was a loud *thump,* and her SUV jolted from an impact. The truck had hit her rear bumper.

5

Kaylee pressed the gas with an involuntary twitch of her foot and lurched forward. Her tires hit a deep puddle, which pulled the Escape toward the ditch. She carefully braked and steered, trying to remember the technique for gaining control of the vehicle. On her side of the road, the ditch was deep and filled with running water that glistened in her headlights.

The tires hit pavement and caught with a jerk, then the car picked up speed. Panting with relief, she realized she and Bear were okay. There would be no going off the road tonight, to end up at the mercy of the menace following them.

The interior of the Escape was abruptly dark. She risked a glance into the rearview and saw that the other vehicle had stopped and was turning around in someone's driveway.

Hands tense on the wheel, Kaylee leaned forward, every atom in her body straining to get home, to reach safety. She finally spotted the white mailbox that marked the drive and pulled in, racing up the dirt lane to Wildflower Cottage.

She parked the car and hurried to unlock the door, then shuttled Bear, her bags, and the crate of papers inside. Once they were all under shelter, she locked the door again.

The next priority was to feed Bear. As he crunched away on his kibble, she placed a call to the police. There was probably zero chance of them finding the vehicle, but she wanted to report the incident in case there was damage to her car.

A wave of nausea swept over her. *Someone hit me on purpose.* She said a quick prayer of thanks that she and Bear hadn't ended up in the gully. She doubted the other driver would have rescued them or even called for help. She'd sensed malice in the relentless glare of those headlights.

"911. What's your emergency?"

As Kaylee made the report to the dispatcher, she realized she probably should have stayed at the scene. But under these conditions, she wouldn't have dared risk it even if she'd had the wherewithal to think of it.

"Where are you now, ma'am?" the dispatcher asked.

"I'm at home. I was too frightened to stop. It seemed like the hit was deliberate."

"Then it's good you kept going. I'll send a deputy out to your house shortly."

While she waited, Kaylee made a fire, allowing herself to relax to the sound of crackling kindling and the warmth soon emanating from the fireplace. Rubbing both arms, she realized she still wore her damp clothes. She dashed for the bedroom and changed into a sweatshirt, cozy fleece yoga pants, and thick wool socks knitted by her grandmother. Then she stationed herself in front of the hearth to wait.

A cruiser pulled into the yard with a crunch of gravel. Kaylee went to the door to wait. Deputies Robyn Garcia and Alan Brooks emerged from the vehicle. Robyn headed for the steps while Alan pulled out a flashlight and examined the rear of the Escape. He crouched down and ran his fingers along the metal.

"Any damage?" Kaylee called. "I didn't have a chance to look."

Deputy Brooks shook his head. "A small dent, that's all. I don't see any paint from the other vehicle. But if the other bumper was unpainted steel, you wouldn't."

"Let's go in and we'll take a report," Deputy Garcia said with a nod, making her ponytail bounce. "The hit-and-run concerns us even if you don't file an insurance claim."

The two deputies shed their rain gear in the entryway and entered the toasty living room. "Have a seat," Kaylee said.

"This is nice." Deputy Garcia moved close to the fireplace. "Especially on a night like this."

"We've already had a couple of accidents," Deputy Brooks said. "Some of the roads are washing out. People are hydroplaning like crazy."

Kaylee shuddered. She'd been only inches from that ditch. "Want coffee? I was going to make some."

"Yes please," Deputy Garcia said for both of them. "It's going to be a long night."

While Kaylee put on a pot of coffee, she answered questions, relaying how the truck or large SUV had come up on her fast and trailed her along the road. "It was really scary when he hit me." She closed her eyes briefly, reliving the horrific moment of impact.

"He?" Deputy Garcia asked sharply. "Did you see the driver?"

"No, I'm afraid not. The headlights were glaring right into my car." Kaylee shrugged. "It could have been a woman. I just said 'he' automatically."

"Do you remember any details about the vehicle?" Deputy Brooks asked. Kaylee shook her head.

By the time the deputies finished their coffee and left, Kaylee knew that the police couldn't do much since she had no real information about the other driver. But it had helped her morale to file a report, even if only a little.

She sat in front of the fire with her half-full mug of coffee, hoping the heat would bake the cold, bone-deep dread out of her body. Who had slammed into her car? Why? Would they try something else?

The wind howled around the eaves, making something bang against the house. She jumped to her feet, causing Bear to give a tiny yip from his position sprawled on the hearth rug.

"It's okay, Bear. Everything is okay." Clenching her fists, she breathed deeply.

Her cell phone shrilled from the end table, displaying a Seattle number without a name. She tucked her hands under her arms, refusing to answer despite Bear's puzzled stare. A few moments later came the ding that announced a message.

"Should I check the message, Bear?" She sighed deeply. "I might as well." Heart in her throat, she pressed the icon and listened.

Boyd Parsons wanted to engage her boat and piloting services the next day for a trip to Blossom Island. "Believe it or not, it's supposed to stop raining," he said. "Please call me in the morning either way, okay? I need to get to that island before I'm scooped." His laugh was as warm and charming as his voice.

Relieved and feeling slightly foolish, Kaylee laughed and plopped back into her chair. "Up for a boat ride, Bear? Let's see if Reese wants to come along." Hopefully he wouldn't mind that their picnic had become a treasure hunt.

6

At the marina the next morning, Kaylee parked next to Reese's pickup truck. He was sitting inside, windows down, listening to the radio. She gave a honk of her horn to attract his attention and rolled down her driver's side window.

He turned off the music. "Hey. Ready for our big adventure?"

"I think so." Kaylee had brought plenty of food, water, and rain gear. Safety equipment was already on the boat, along with maps and compass, although the *KayBea* had a GPS system. Was there anything she was forgetting? She hadn't been out in the boat for months.

Reese laughed. "Come on, captain. You'll need to do better than that for your poor passengers." A certified United States Power Squadron instructor, Reese had schooled Kaylee in marine safety prior to her obtaining a license. He grabbed a backpack from the cargo area, locked up the truck, and joined Kaylee, who was unloading the Escape. "Let's head down to the boat and go through the predeparture checklist."

"Yes, teacher," she said, giving him a teasing smile. She pointed to a heavy cooler. "As I recall, a big lunch is item number one. Can you please bring that for me?"

"Sure thing." He grabbed the handles and hefted the cooler with a grunt. "What's in here? Ballast?"

"No, but the water bottles can double as flotation once they're empty," she quipped.

By the time Boyd and Kathy arrived in a tan sedan, Kaylee and Reese had checked the engine and other equipment, tested the radio, and made sure they had flares, tow rope, and life preservers on board. Bear sported his orange canine life jacket, one of the first things Kaylee had bought for the *KayBea*.

Both writer and librarian were dressed appropriately for the cool, overcast day, wearing rubber-soled boots, jeans, and sweaters. Boyd carried a duffel bag in one hand, and his free arm was draped around Kathy's shoulders.

"So that's the famous author," Reese murmured as the couple trudged across the marina parking lot. "They're awfully friendly for ex-spouses."

Kaylee had to agree with his assessment. "I hope Kathy doesn't get hurt again." She waved to attract their attention. "Over here."

Kathy pointed and they changed direction toward the proper gangway. "Good morning," Boyd said with a grin as they reached the *KayBea's* tie-up on the floating dock. He dropped his bag onto the dock and held out a hand to Reese. "Boyd Parsons."

"Reese Holt." Reese shook his hand. "Welcome aboard." He reached out to Kathy. "Hi, Kathy. Let me help you."

The two men began to trade remarks about the weather outlook and the boat.

Kathy turned to Kaylee, eyes sparkling. "I love your boat. Do you go out a lot?"

"Not as much as I should," Kaylee said. "But I'm lucky to have it. It used to be my grandfather's." She moved Boyd's duffel to a safe spot and then placed Kathy's backpack next to it. "I brought extra rain gear in case you need it."

Kathy sat on the bench seat next to Bear. "So did we." She tipped her head back and scanned the sky. "Hopefully the rain will hold off until we get back."

"I hope so too," Kaylee said. The center console had a canopy, but it wouldn't protect them all.

Bear nuzzled Kathy's hand and she laughed. "What a sweetie." She began to pat the dog, who crawled into the librarian's lap and curled up. "Speaking of sweeties." She wiggled her eyebrows. "What's the story with Reese?"

Kaylee flushed, darting a glance toward the carpenter. Thankfully he and Boyd were engrossed in a conversation about the previous baseball season, no doubt triggered by Reese's Dodgers cap. She shrugged. "We're friends."

Kathy's smile was smug. "Uh-huh. I'm sure."

Thankfully Kaylee was saved from further embarrassment by Reese, who called out, "Captain, it's time to launch."

"That's my cue." Kaylee joined the men at the console. "Before we set off, can you fill us in a little, Boyd? What are we looking for on Blossom Island?"

The writer crossed his arms across his broad chest and leaned against the rail. "There were four men involved in the bank robbery. Two of them went to jail. One of them, Lester Clayton, was shot by the police—right here on Orcas Island."

Reese's eyes lit up. He enjoyed puzzles from history. "So what happened to the fourth?"

Boyd shook his head. "No one knows. But I did talk to a descendant of one of the men who went to jail. His great-grandfather was arrested almost immediately after the robbery, along with his companion. But Lester and the other man, Jack Butler, escaped with the loot."

"That's confirmation the money might have made it out to the islands," Kaylee said, excited.

"Exactly. The original plan was for the men to meet up on Blossom Island, then make a break for Canada. But as we know, Lester went to Orcas. The burning question is, what happened on Blossom?"

"And why did Lester go to Orcas?" Kaylee added. If he hadn't, would he have made it to Canada with the money? He might have lived to a ripe old age, a fugitive but among the living.

"I haven't figured that part out yet," Boyd admitted. "Hopefully it will unfold for us. All we can do is take one step at a time."

Kathy patted his arm. "Between the two of us, we'll get there." She winked at Reese and Kaylee. "Nothing like having your own personal research librarian, is there?"

Boyd smiled down at her. "I couldn't have gotten this far without you."

What would happen when he reached his goal? Would he discard Kathy—again? Kaylee shook off her uneasiness, again thinking it wasn't her business. "So Blossom Island it is," she said. "I've already got the coordinates plugged in." She turned the key and the finely tuned engine roared to life. Then she deftly backed the boat out of the slip and headed toward the mouth of the harbor.

Although the day was damp and cool, the water was smooth, the air still. The boat skimmed across the silver water, the islands around them covered in evergreens and mystery. Over on the mainland, Mount Baker's white peak gleamed above a fringe of clouds.

"I love being on the water," Kaylee said to Reese, leaning close so she could be heard over the roar of the engine. "I should come out here more often." She got so caught up in her daily life and the responsibilities of her business. While she enjoyed them thoroughly, it was good to take a break and get out in the natural world, to soak in its beauty and peace.

Standing with arms folded and legs braced against the boat's movement, Reese threw her a grin. "Me too. We'll have to do it more often." He eyed the gray sky. "Next spring."

"Yes, we probably won't make it out again this year." But her heart warmed at the thought of venturing out to explore the San Juan Islands with Reese. It was definitely something to look forward to over the long winter ahead.

Blossom Island wasn't far, an islet located to the east of Orcas

Island, tucked among a group of other small islands. Kaylee had researched it online and learned it was about five acres in size, partially wooded, and home to nesting gulls. The only place to land was on the north side, in a sheltered cove.

Slowing the engine, Kaylee slipped into the cove, carefully maneuvering through outcroppings of rocks. Although the boat glided gently, its presence caused clusters of gulls and seabirds to rise into the air with cries and squawks. The island had a tiny slice of beach covered with pebbles, mud, and driftwood, so Kaylee was able to anchor the boat close to shore.

"This is as close as I dare to get," she said. "But we can step out on those rocks." She pointed to a convenient outcropping.

While the disturbed birds continued to wheel overhead, the treasure hunters climbed out of the boat, Boyd lugging his duffel bag and Reese bringing water bottles in his pack. Kaylee carried Bear, leash attached, and set him on the ground. He immediately pulled, wanting to explore all the new smells. After a futile attempt to settle him down, she gave in and let him roam to every corner of the beach on the leash.

Meanwhile, Boyd unzipped his bag and pulled out a metal detector, a digital camera, a notebook, and a topographic map in a waterproof case.

"What's the plan of attack, boss?" Reese asked eagerly. Kaylee could tell the excitement had gotten to him regardless of his concern about Boyd and Kathy.

Boyd unfolded the map on a nearby boulder and Kaylee hurried over with Bear. "We're here." Boyd touched a spot on the map, then moved his finger a short distance inland. "And this is where the cabin is located. I'm going to use the metal detector in a radius around the cabin, moving outward. But if they used a canvas sack instead of a metal cashbox, we're probably out of luck."

"What can I do to help?" Kathy asked.

"How are you at taking pictures?" Boyd handed her the digital camera. "I want you to photograph everything: the cabin, the surroundings, anything we find. You never know what will come in handy later."

Kathy took the camera and slung the cord around her neck. "I think I can do that." The expression on her face was both nervous and excited.

"Of course you can." Boyd gave her a reassuring smile. He foraged around in the duffel and pulled out a folding shovel and a short pickax. "Reese, can you take these, please?" Then he picked up the metal detector. "Ready, everyone?"

They allowed the writer to lead the way across the beach and up a narrow trail into the woods. This was beaten down enough to reveal that other people probably came to the island now and then. Kaylee spotted telltale cans and papers in the woods, trash left by less-than-conscientious visitors.

They entered a small clearing and found the cabin, constructed of wide boards and roofed with mossy wood shingles. Amazingly, most of the window glass was intact, although the sagging porch and roofline revealed the structure's age and deterioration.

"Jack's family lived here for a while in the early 1920s," Boyd said. "His father was a fisherman. By the time of the bank robbery in 1935, it had been empty for a decade."

"So that's why he and Lester came here," Kathy said. "Jack knew the place."

"That makes sense to me." Boyd nodded.

Lured by curiosity, Kaylee moved toward the cabin. She stepped onto the single stone step, then put an experimental foot on the porch.

"Be careful," Reese warned, hurrying to her side.

"It looks okay," Kaylee said, backing down. She reined in Bear, who was already up there sniffing around.

Reese tested the porch with one foot, pressing slowly and carefully. "I think it's all right." He put up a hand. "I'll try it first."

While Kaylee and the others watched, he crossed the porch and opened the creaky door. After peering inside, he gestured. "I think it's fine. Let's go in."

Kaylee and Bear were next, after Reese. Kathy held the camera in readiness and Boyd brought up the rear. He glanced around at every detail, even inhaling deeply of the dusty smell of dry wood inside. Kaylee had the sense he was collecting mental details for his book.

"Must be a good roof," Reese said, craning his neck to check the rafters. The cabin was one large room, with a loft at one side. It was dim inside due to the daylight filtering through dirty windows and surrounding trees.

"Oh my." Kathy cringed in disgust. "I can't believe people lived here."

Kaylee had to agree that the cabin was pretty dismal. The only furniture was a pine table with two chairs and an ancient sofa, both covered in deep layers of dust. A rusty cast-iron stove had once provided both heat and a cooking surface. A hand pump next to a stained porcelain sink was the only plumbing.

Reese gingerly climbed up the ladder to the loft. "Nothing up here but an ancient mattress."

"Check this out." Boyd picked up a rusty but colorful spice can from the windowsill over the sink. "It's got to be over eighty years old." Several other cans—coffee, other spices, and pepper—lined the sill. "Kathy, could you get some pictures?"

"Sure." Kathy went around and snapped photos of everything in the cabin.

Once they had explored every corner, Boyd began operating the metal detector, assisted by Kathy. At Boyd's request, Reese and Kaylee set off into the woods to see if there was anything of interest nearby.

"It's so peaceful out here," Reese said as they trod on a quiet woodland path, fir trees towering overhead.

Kaylee took a deep breath of *Pseudotsuga menziesii* and salt-scented air. She heard only the gentle sigh of wind in the Douglas fir trees and the faint hush of the ocean. "It's definitely quiet." Bear jerked forward on his leash, whining. "Well, except for that."

The little dog was stronger than he appeared and Kaylee found herself almost running behind him. He stopped in a gully between two huge trees and began to dig.

Reese laughed. "Maybe he's found the treasure." Then he examined the rusty item Bear sent rolling. "That's an old tin can. This must be a bottle dump."

The dog's flailing paws sent something else onto the ground near Kaylee's boot. She bent to pick it up. "This is no tin can." It was a pocket watch.

The implications hit her as she turned it over in her hands.

"Reese." Kaylee's voice sounded strangled, even to her own ears. "Look at this."

He took the soil-encrusted watch and examined it, front and back. Then he glanced at the dump, where Bear was still happily digging away, exposing more cans and a few bottles. "Who would throw away a watch?"

"They wouldn't." The find sent chills down Kaylee's spine. "What else do you suppose is down there?"

"I don't know, but we should probably stop Bear from digging until we find out." Reese handed her the watch. "I'm going to get Boyd and his metal detector over here."

Kaylee hauled a resistant Bear away from the alluring trash heap and sat on a boulder nearby. She brushed at the dirt covering the watch, then stopped. An expert should clean it.

Boyd, Kathy, and Reese came crashing through the woods.

"You found a watch?" Boyd asked, radiating excitement. He reached his hand out. "Let me see."

Kaylee handed it over, and Kathy leaned close and peered at the object in Boyd's palm.

He gave it back to Kaylee. "Interesting. That's a bottle dump?"

Reese picked up the tin can. "That's my guess. Most old places have them since they didn't exactly have trash pickup or recycling back then."

"Especially out here on the islands." Boyd paced about, rubbing his chin. "Let me try the metal detector and see if anything big is down there." He grinned. "A pile of garbage would be a great place to hide money."

The other three watched while Boyd turned on his machine and scanned the forest floor. Since there was a lot of metal underground, the detector kept signaling. The most active area was where Bear had been digging, which didn't surprise Kaylee. No doubt some odors still lingered, and he'd picked them up with his sensitive nose.

"I'm getting a good reading here," Boyd said. "Let's see what we can find."

Reese fetched the tools and the two men began to dig, Boyd with the shovel and Reese going through heaps of cans and bottles with the pickax. They'd been doing that for fifteen minutes when Boyd grunted and bent to pick up something.

"What is that?" Kathy asked, squinting to see the rectangular object.

"It's a man's belt buckle." Boyd's eyes darted to the watch Kaylee still held and then back to the buckle. His mouth set in a grim line. "It's only a hunch, but judging by these two items, I think we might have found Jack Butler's grave."

7

Kathy gasped. "Jack Butler?" Her eyes widened as she pointed at the bottle dump. "You mean his skeleton is under there?" She sat abruptly on a nearby tree stump.

"If you really think that, Boyd," Reese said, "we'd better call the sheriff's office. They'll need to take care of it from here."

The writer's brow creased. "You're absolutely right. But as a writer I have to say . . ." He shook a fist at the dump, then flashed the group a rueful grin. "There goes my exclusive."

As a scientist, Kaylee could sympathize. She'd been scooped once or twice when another botanist figured out something first. "At least you're the one who found Jack, we think. No one can take that away."

Boyd nodded. "True. And who's to say the treasure was ever here? Lester might have taken it with him to Orcas. I haven't finished searching the property at Buttercup Cottage."

Kaylee remembered Edna's papers. "I've been meaning to mention this. Edna used to have her business in my shop on Main Street. I found a box of paperwork in my attic." She shrugged. "I don't know if anything important is in there, but I'll let you look."

"Thanks, Kaylee. That whole situation is a mystery too. Why involve Edna? Was it random or on purpose?"

"I vote for romance," Kathy said from her seat on the stump.

Reese studied the sky. "Let's get the sheriff out here before the weather gets bad." He pulled out his phone. "No signal. Guess we'll have to use the boat radio."

Under Reese's watchful eye, Kaylee got ready to place the call, tuning to a private police operator channel at his suggestion.

"You don't need to broadcast to the entire world," he said. "It's not truly an emergency either."

Boyd appeared slightly relieved. "Good. I was picturing boats streaming here from every direction."

"Oh, they'll be here later," Kathy said, folding her arms. "Once word gets out." She glanced back up the hill. "Let's go take more photographs before they get here."

She and Boyd disappeared up the trail. "Hope they don't disturb anything," Reese muttered.

"You can go after them," Kaylee said. "I'll be fine." But Reese didn't budge, watching as she called the operator. She gave her coordinates and said, "I'd like to request assistance. We've found, um, a potential human burial site in an old bottle dump."

"Native American?" the operator asked. There were strict laws about disturbing any of those sites.

"No, it's more recent. It may involve a murder from 1935."

Even over the airwaves, Kaylee could sense the operator's curiosity, but he merely said, "I'll send a boat ASAP. We have someone patrolling in the area."

Kaylee thanked the operator and hung up the handset. "Hopefully it won't be too long before they get here."

"Why don't you go update those two?" Reese suggested, nodding in the direction Boyd and Kathy had gone. "I'll stay here and wait."

"Okay. We'll be right back." Kaylee and Bear headed into the woods, the little dog running ahead on his leash. Once again, Kaylee was struck by how peaceful it was on the tiny island. What had happened here all those decades ago? Had Lester killed his partner so he could have all the money? If so, why hadn't he hightailed it to Canada? Instead he'd gone to his death on Orcas.

Kathy and Boyd were huddled together near the bottle dump, whispering. When Boyd gave Kathy a kiss on the cheek, Kaylee halted, feeling very much like a third wheel. Then Bear barked at a squirrel and the couple turned, moving apart.

"Any news?" Boyd asked.

"The marine patrol will be here shortly." Kaylee moved closer to the dump. Had another area been disturbed? "Did you find anything else?"

The expression of guilt that crossed Kathy's face was a dead giveaway. "We did poke around a little. Not anywhere near where we found the watch or buckle, though."

Boyd opened his hand. A gold coin sat on his palm. "It's a 1906, two-and-one-half dollar coin. Worth a lot more than that these days."

Kaylee's heart gave a thud. "Were there gold coins stolen in the robbery?"

"A few. Mostly bills." Boyd's fingers closed around the coin. "You two are my witnesses I found this here." He gave a longing glance at the ground, plainly wishing he could continue the excavation.

"You dug it up with your toe," Kathy said. "I'll vouch for that."

Kaylee had the feeling Kathy would firmly stand behind Boyd, no matter what. She heard the rumble of an engine in the cove. "I think the marine patrol is here."

A few minutes later, Reese came up the path, followed by two men in uniform. The taller of the two nodded to the small group waiting by the bottle dump. "I'm Deputy Varney and this is Deputy Jones." Varney wore his head shaved and had the stiff demeanor of a former military man. Jones was shorter and stout. His lank black hair and tanned complexion spoke to his Quinault ancestry.

Kaylee introduced herself, followed by Kathy and Boyd. "You might have heard of me," Boyd said. He named the books he'd written.

The two deputies exchanged glances. Varney scratched his

head with a doubtful expression. "I may have. Does this have something to do with why we were called out here?"

Boyd was unperturbed by the deputy's skepticism. "Actually, yes. I'm writing a book about the Seattle bank robbery of 1935. Do you recall the shootout on Orcas?"

"My grandfather used to talk about it," Jones said. "How does Blossom Island fit in?"

The writer appeared smug. "It's not common knowledge, but the two robbers who escaped, Lester Clayton and Jack Butler, stopped here first. This was supposed to be the rendezvous spot for the four involved, but two were arrested in Seattle. Clayton was shot a few days later, but no trace of Butler was ever found." He paused to let the deputies absorb this.

Varney sighed. "So, judging by the call we got, you think Jack Butler is buried here."

"Exactly," Kathy said. "Boyd brought his metal detector over here so we could look for the bank loot, but Kaylee's dog found a pocket watch."

Everyone's head swiveled toward Bear, who was busy scratching an ear. He glanced up as though to say, "What?"

"Boyd found a belt buckle in the same spot." Kaylee pointed it out. "We didn't think it was a good idea to keep digging."

"Good call," Varney said. "There might be nothing here or . . ." He didn't need to finish the statement. "You have some tools, I see." He picked up the shovel.

Jones made a shooing motion. "Why don't you all stand over there while we work?"

The group from Orcas Island moved a distance away, to a spot where a fallen log made a natural seat. "Why don't I go get our lunch?" Reese asked. "I could use something to eat."

"Let me go with you," Kaylee said. "There's too much for one person to carry."

Kathy squealed. "Eat while the deputies dig up a body?" She gave an exaggerated shudder. "No thanks."

"I brought a thermos of coffee and cookies from Death by Chocolate," Kaylee said with a smile. "Those might tempt you."

Boyd rubbed his hands together. "I could use some coffee, thanks. It's chilly out here." The gray clouds had thickened and with them came a nagging little breeze.

Kaylee and Reese trudged down to the boat. Once out of earshot, Kaylee said, "Boyd found a gold coin in the dump."

Reese's brows rose. "Maybe they did bury the money there."

"Could be. I'm not sure he was going to tell me about it, but Kathy's face gave it away." Kaylee laughed. "She definitely doesn't have a poker face. Even under whatever spell Boyd has cast on her."

"If I was Boyd right now, I wouldn't be very happy," Reese said. "He's not going to be able to keep his story under wraps if they did find Jack Butler up there."

"True. Unless he can figure out how to spin the story even bigger somehow, for book sales." *Finding the treasure would do that.* Kaylee foraged in her bags and pulled out the thermos, paper cups, and pastries. "There are sandwiches in the cooler. Do you want to grab those and some bottles of water?"

Reese took a peek at the grinders from the deli at Blenham's Market, which had ingredient notations written on the white wrapping paper. "Excellent choices, Kaylee. I'm starving."

"I figured an outing in the fresh air would make people hungry." She smiled ruefully. "Of course I had no idea we'd find a potential grave site."

Back at the bottle dump, Kaylee poured cups of coffee and let the others choose what they wanted. Despite her protests of not being able to eat, Kathy split a turkey grinder with Boyd, and Reese grabbed an Italian sub.

Kaylee had barely bitten into her roast beef sandwich when Jones gave a shout. They'd uncovered human bones.

The call went out for backup, and Orcas Island's Sheriff Eddie Maddox was among the first to arrive. When Kaylee spotted his familiar stride coming up the path, she felt her heart rate slow. Smart, fair, and calm, Eddie was a good man to have on a case.

He stopped in front of their little group, hands on hips, nodding a greeting. His eyes were curious when they rested on Boyd. "I understand you stumbled on a grave site. Want to tell me how that happened?"

Since Boyd had initiated the excursion, the others let him explain. "I have good reason to believe that our skeleton is Jack Butler," Boyd said in conclusion. "He disappeared after the robbery and was never seen again."

Maddox tilted his head and studied Boyd, his dark eyes gleaming. "There's no mention of Blossom Island in any accounts of the robbery and its aftermath."

"I know." Boyd's expression was rueful. "I learned about it during an interview with one of the other robber's descendants. Jack's family thought he'd escaped to Canada, but they never heard from him again." He gestured. "How could they?"

Boyd was a good storyteller, Kaylee had to give him that.

The sheriff pivoted to stare at the site, where a forensics team was now carefully excavating the skeleton. "I guess we'll see, once we identify the remains."

"If he's wearing a ruby ring on his pinky, then it's Jack." Boyd pulled out his phone and flipped through photographs until he found the one he wanted. He held it out for the sheriff to see. "He always wore that ring."

Sheriff Maddox didn't react, but Kaylee could tell he was filing away the information. "We'll take this under advisement. I'll need you all to stay here a little longer. We may have more questions for you."

"Will you keep me in the loop?" Boyd asked. "I can be of help to you with what I know. A consultant of sorts. In return, I'd love any details you can share."

Maddox's gaze grew cold at Boyd's forward manner. "We'll see, Mr. Parsons."

After he strode away, Kathy reached for the phone. "I want to see." She studied the picture, then passed it on to Reese. When the phone came around to Kaylee, she saw Jack Butler had been an attractive man. In the black-and-white photograph, he was standing in a cocky stance, leaning against a Ford automobile with arms folded. The large, ornate ring on his right hand was clearly visible.

What led him to crime? Kaylee wondered. The long-lasting Depression had driven many to despair. Had Jack, Lester, and the others decided to take their financial futures into their own hands?

While the police crew worked on, Kaylee and her friends decided to take Bear for a stroll around the island. They checked out the colonies of seabirds—who didn't appreciate Bear's intrusion—and the variety of natural plant life, including finding a patch of *Camassia quamash*, blue camas, now gone to seed. "The bulbs were a staple for the tribes who lived on these islands," Kaylee explained to the others. "Even Lewis and Clark relied on them during their trip West."

Kathy gave a curious look. "How do you tell which plants are good to eat? I'm always afraid to try foraging."

"Good question." Kaylee enjoyed sharing her knowledge with eager students. "Come with me." She led them to a group of similar plants. "This is *Zigadenus venenosus*, better known as the death camas." After their exclamations of shock, she said, "See how the seedpods are different in size and position on the stalk? Dead giveaway. No pun intended." Bear was sniffing the plant curiously and she gently tugged him back. "No, Bear. Don't dig up these bulbs."

Reese regarded Kaylee with admiration. "I'll definitely bring you along if I ever need to live off the land."

Boyd was taking notes on his tablet. "Fascinating. I understand you were a forensic botanist for the Seattle police, Dr. Bleu."

He must have checked her out. Kaylee didn't know whether to be flattered or disturbed. "I enjoyed using my knowledge to solve cases," she said. "I've done some of that in a small way on Orcas."

"More than small, I'd say," Reese said, then checked the time. "It's been a while. Let's head back and see if they've made any progress."

"I sure hope so," Kathy said. "I'm ready to go, I think. Enough excitement for one day."

By the time they reached the bottle dump again, Sheriff Maddox had news. "We've uncovered the skeleton. It's male, and he's wearing a ruby pinky ring." His expression was grim. "Looks like Jack Butler all right, Mr. Parsons."

Boyd's eyes glinted briefly before he visibly tamped down his excitement. "What was the cause of death? Could you tell?"

Maddox sighed. "The .38 caliber bullet floating in the rib cage kind of gave it away. Jack Butler was shot."

A short while later, they were cleared to leave, although Boyd would have loved to hang around all night. He satisfied himself by writing notes in his tablet as they walked back to the boat.

"I can't wait to get home," Reese whispered to Kaylee when they reached the rocky beach.

"Me neither." To Kaylee's eyes, the familiar *KayBea* looked like halfway there already. "Being here reminds me of *Gilligan's Island*." She laughed and he joined her.

Kathy came up beside them. "I sure hope that fog lifts or we'll never get back to Orcas."

Kaylee followed Kathy's gaze and noticed to her dismay that mist was settling in over the islands. "Oh no. We'd better hurry."

"Don't worry about it," Reese said. "You've got navigation equipment on board. We'll be fine."

"I hope so," Kaylee whispered, too low for him to hear. The prospect of piloting a boat in fog for the first time was tying her stomach into knots of anxiety and dread.

Working on autopilot, her mind occupied by the challenge ahead, Kaylee helped load the boat and went through the checklist with Reese. With one eye, she kept watch over the thickening fog, which was spreading over the glassy water like smoke. The sun was also sinking behind the clouds, so they were losing what little daylight they had.

With Kaylee at the helm, they navigated out of the cove, avoiding the police craft now sharing the small area. She checked the instruments and set her course for Turtle Cove.

"Next stop, the marina," she sang out over the engine when they reached open water. "Hold on, everyone."

But a short distance into the bay, the treacherous fog came down like a blanket, obscuring visibility and muffling sound. Kaylee's anxiety ratcheted up as she feverishly tried to remember the protocol. "Reduce speed," she said quietly. That was a given. There was something else . . . oh yes, horn every two minutes. She set the equipment.

The first time the horn went off, everyone jumped. "Sorry," Kaylee said. "It's the law."

Reese nodded in approval. "Good call, Kaylee. Hopefully we'll be through this fog bank soon."

Seated next to Boyd on the bench seat, Kathy put her hands over her ears. "Me too."

Boyd patted her knee with a laugh. "Better deaf than rammed by another boat."

As though conjured by his words, a dark shape loomed up in the mist, drifting out from behind a rocky islet. No lights shone, and only the low rumble of the engine provided a warning.

The other craft was headed straight for the *KayBea*.

8

"Craft approaching on your port side," Reese called.

"I see it," Kaylee shouted back. She studied the trajectory of the oncoming boat while manually sounding the horn. It was a fishing boat about the same size as the *KayBea,* which meant she had the right of way—if they would give it. It was moving pretty fast, narrowing the distance every second. In response, she cut the engine even more and pulled hard to the right, fighting a strong current and the rising tide.

She blasted the horn again but the other boat continued on its set course, seeming not to see or hear them. Boyd, Kathy, and Reese joined the fray, adding their shouts between the earsplitting honks.

As the boat drew closer, Kaylee saw two figures draped in rain gear standing behind the wheel. They stared straight ahead, not reacting to the *KayBea's* signs of distress. A chill ran down her spine.

Are they doing this on purpose? It certainly seemed that way. Kaylee wrenched the wheel again, sending her boat toward a rocky outcropping. Now she had two obstacles to avoid.

A rush of fear almost swamped her. The *KayBea* was going to sink with four people and a beloved dog on board, in foggy conditions and far from help. Then a burst of anger flashed over her. She snatched up the radio, ready to report reckless operation of a watercraft. She had the button pressed when the other boat finally changed direction, ramped up the engine, and roared away.

This averted a collision but created a wake that hit the *KayBea* broadside, making the boat rock violently side to side.

She dropped the radio microphone and wrestled with the wheel, trying to stabilize the boat. Reese leaped to help, applying his muscle and skill.

At last, the *KayBea* was stable and safely underway again. Kaylee set the course for home and sagged against the console, sucking in deep breaths. "Thank you, Reese. I couldn't have done it without you."

"Whew. That was a challenge all right." Reese wiped his forearm across his face. "I thought we might end up on those rocks."

A white-faced Boyd joined them. "Am I crazy, or did that other boat do that on purpose? It really seemed like they were going to ram us."

"That's what I thought," Kaylee said. "They didn't even look over when we were shouting and blowing the horn."

"Those bums must have been deaf." Kathy's expression was such a perfect picture of justified outrage that Kaylee laughed. Then she couldn't stop laughing. She bent double, giggling helplessly. Tears sprang to her eyes and dripped down her cheeks. Knowing how foolish she must appear—in front of a best-selling author, no less—only made her laugh more.

She felt a strong hand grip her elbow. "Come sit down, Kaylee. You need a snack and a break." Reese settled her on the bench seat, then foraged for the cookies and thermos of coffee.

Boyd was at the helm, Kathy snuggled up near his elbow.

"I asked. He's experienced," Reese said. "Plus, we're coming out of the fog so we should be all right." As he spoke, the fog bank became wisps drifting skyward, revealing the late afternoon sun breaking through the clouds.

Kaylee accepted a cup of coffee and a big chocolate chip cookie. Bear jumped up and sat close beside her, licking his chops in hope of a dropped crumb. "No, Bear. This cookie isn't good for you." Kaylee found a dog biscuit in her jacket pocket and gave it to him. "Did you see the registration or name on that boat?" she asked Reese. She sipped the coffee gratefully, feeling its warmth revive her spirits. "I was too busy to notice."

"I didn't." Reese sat on the seat beside her. He selected a cookie and took a big bite. "I think they might have been covered up."

"Who does that?" Kaylee silently answered her own question. The look Reese gave her confirmed he was thinking the same thing: A person trying to disguise their identity. "I was ready to call the marine patrol when they veered off." She ate some cookie. "Maybe I should report it anyway."

That would make the second call to the sheriff's department in as many days, not counting the call to Blossom Island for the human remains. At least this time she hadn't been hit. That would have been disastrous out on the water.

"I wish we had more details to report. Otherwise they really can't do anything."

Kaylee stood, refreshed enough to take over the wheel again. She'd better be the one to bring them into harbor. "Thanks, Boyd," she said. "I appreciate the break."

He relinquished the controls with a smile. "No problem. As a thank-you, I'd like to take you out to dinner. How does O'Brien's sound?"

O'Brien's was a popular restaurant right on the harbor. "It sounds great," Kaylee said. "What a nice offer." The idea of not cooking dinner after the long day they'd had was really appealing.

"I'd like to treat you too, Reese, if you're available," Boyd said.

Reese grinned. "You had me at O'Brien's. Love that place."

Boyd checked his phone. "Let's meet at seven. That will give us time to change our clothes and relax for a bit."

"That will work," Kaylee said. "I have to take Bear home first. It's too cold to sit outside." She enjoyed sitting on O'Brien's dog-friendly patio when weather permitted.

The harbor soon came into view, lights twinkling in the early dusk. Docking the boat in its slip felt like coming home. Kaylee breathed out a huge sigh of relief, feeling the tension leave her shoulders. "Here we are, folks. Turtle Cove."

The parking lot at O'Brien's was pretty full for a November weeknight. Kaylee slid the Escape into a spot between two pickup trucks, reflecting that patronage by locals was a sure sign of good value. Savvy island businesses didn't focus only on serving tourists, who came and went with the seasons.

Inside, the restaurant was full of steamy warmth, chatter, and the clatter of dishes. Reese's hand went up from a booth in the back and, with a word to the hostess, Kaylee wound through the tables to join her friends. On the way, she enjoyed the sea-themed decorations—the nets hanging from the ceiling, the brass lanterns over each booth, and the pictures and stuffed fish hanging on the walls.

Boyd and Kathy sat across from Reese, and all three were studying the menu. They looked up with smiles when she slid into the booth. "It's getting chilly out there," Kaylee said by way of greeting. "I'm glad we made it in before full dark."

Boyd's mouth tightened. "I'm thankful we made it back, period. That ride back was a little too exciting, even for me."

Kathy gaped at him. "I thought you thrived on danger. You said that you took risks with every book. That it went with the territory of true crime."

The author shook his head. "I never had friends involved before. That's what has me spooked. Plus, this is a cold case, an eighty-year-old robbery and murder. Who cares about that?"

"Anyone searching for the treasure." Reese's voice was deliberately low. He smiled at the waitress hurrying up to their table. "Are we ready to order?"

Kaylee and Kathy ordered bowls of chowder and house salads while Reese had a burger and Boyd a fish sandwich.

As their server left to put in their requests, the hostess brushed past their booth with two men in tow. As they passed, Kaylee recognized them as the bird-watchers she'd been seeing all over town. She gave them a nod of greeting and said hello. In return, both men silently studied Kaylee and her companions. They settled in the next booth, and the hostess ran through the specials.

"Who were those men?" Reese asked. "Customers of yours?"

Kaylee opened her tea bag and set it to steep in the hot water the waitress had brought. "No, they're tourists. I ran into them at the farm."

An older local fisherman named Clay Tucker shuffled up to their booth. "Hey, are you that writer guy?" he asked Boyd.

Boyd threw his tablemates an amused glance. He sat up a little straighter. "If you're asking if I'm Boyd Parsons, then yes I am."

Clay waved that off. "I heard you found a skeleton on Blossom Island today. Is it true it was one of those bank robbers?" Clay was speaking quite loudly, and his question attracted the attention of nearby diners.

"Here we go," Boyd muttered. He rubbed his chin, considering Clay's question. "What does the sheriff's office say?"

"That's just it—they won't say who it was." Clay threw up both hands in exasperation. "But I heard you were on the island, so I'm asking you."

Whoever had informed Clay was in the know. Was it one of the sheriff's deputies? Or had gossip already spread through the grapevine?

A tiny smile flitted across Boyd's lips. "If they won't say, I can't either. Wouldn't want to compromise an investigation." He bent forward and peered behind Clay. "I hate to cut this short, but our meal is arriving." He held out a hand. "Nice to meet you, Mr. . . . ?"

The older man took his hand with a grumble. "Clay Tucker. I fish around here." He ducked aside as the waitress came up with a loaded tray and headed back to his seat.

The hot food smelled wonderful. Kaylee took a moment to appreciate her meal before picking up her spoon and digging in. The rich chowder was savory, flavored perfectly by onions, butter, and flakes of tender white fish.

On the other side of the table, Boyd and Kathy were enjoying their food with murmurs of appreciation. "Great pick," Boyd said. "I'd forgotten how good this place is."

At the mention of his former time on the island, there was a tiny lull. Then Kathy laughed. "Here on Orcas, everything improves with age."

"I'll agree with that." Reese held up his drink in a salute. His eyes cut to Kaylee and she elbowed him.

"Don't include me in that remark," she huffed, pretending to be offended. They all laughed.

"What's your next move, Boyd?" Reese asked. "The island was a bust regarding the treasure, right?"

Boyd sighed. "Yes, although I can't complain about finding Jack Butler. That will add a lot to the story." He picked up his fish sandwich and took a bite, then wiped his mouth with a napkin. "I'm going to check the outbuildings at Buttercup Cottage next. Those used to have animals living in them, so I kind of put them on the back burner."

"You mean cows?" Kaylee asked.

"Cows, chickens, and sheep, according to what I can tell by the stalls." Boyd shrugged. "It wouldn't be my first choice to bury money in a manure pile, but it would deter thieves, I suppose. Well, other thieves."

Kaylee had to agree with his conclusion. Hopefully all signs of animal occupation were long gone by now. "I can bring you the box of Edna's paperwork tomorrow morning if you want," she offered. "I don't have to be at the shop until late morning."

Boyd bestowed a warm smile on Kaylee. "That would be wonderful. You never know where you might find an important piece of information."

A middle-aged couple came up to the table. "Are you that writer?" the woman asked in a shrill voice. "I heard you found a dead body today."

After putting them off the same way he'd put off Clay Tucker, Boyd waved his hand for the waitress and said, "Let's take the rest of our meal to go."

Kaylee awoke to a world muffled in cotton wool. Overnight, the fog had crept silently in and blanketed the island. She let Bear out and fed him, grabbed a quick breakfast, and then loaded Edna's crate into the car. Bear came along for the long ride over to Buttercup Cottage.

Due to the fog, Kaylee kept her speed below the limit, at times slowing to a crawl. Now and then, the cloud bank thinned, revealing a sparkling blue ocean under sunny skies. They had a nice day to look forward to when the fog lifted.

She passed through Eastsound, buzzing with school and work traffic, and then out onto the other peninsula. She had almost reached Madrona Grove Road when a tiny blue sedan approached from the other direction, moving too fast for the conditions. Kaylee slowed and edged over slightly, annoyed at the other driver's foolhardy driving.

As the vehicle sped past, she recognized Kathy at the wheel. What was she doing out here? The obvious answer was visiting Boyd, although it was pretty early for a social call. Maybe she had wanted to see him before she started work at the library.

Kaylee reached Madrona Grove Road and headed down it. This time, instead of steering into the farm entrance, she kept going. Boyd had said the next driveway led to his cottage.

Sure enough, a faded painted sign ahead read *Buttercup Cottage*. She steered up the rutted driveway, slowing to navigate the rocks and ruts threatening her undercarriage. The woods pressed close and then opened up again, revealing a quaint yellow cottage set among overgrown flower beds. As she drove closer, she saw the paint was peeling and the roof sagged, but the general impression was pleasant and welcoming.

The tan sedan she recognized as Boyd's sat on the side, near the glassed-in sunporch. She pulled up beside it and turned off the engine.

All was still. Not even a bird sang on this misty morning. She let Bear out of the car and he immediately began barking, breaking the restful silence.

"Bear, shush," she said. "You'll disturb people." It wasn't like him to bark without provocation, but maybe he'd caught the odor of a squirrel or even a deer. After clipping Bear onto a leash, Kaylee made her way toward the sunporch. Perhaps Boyd could retrieve the crate from the car, since it was rather heavy. She'd already lugged it down from the shop attic, to her house, and now across the island.

The door to the house was open slightly so she knocked, then put her head in and called. No answer. Peering around, she saw breakfast dishes next to the sink and a half-full carafe on the coffeemaker, which was still on.

Bear pawed at the door, trying to go inside. "I don't think he's in the house," she told him, remembering what he'd said the previous evening. "Let's check the outbuildings."

Boyd wasn't in the barn, which was barely large enough to hold one automobile or half a dozen cows. Beyond several gnarled apple trees, she saw another small wooden building. As she trudged through tall, wet grass, she wondered if these trees had once belonged to the farm next door. The withered apples hanging from the branches or lying in the grass looked similar to the ones Paul grew.

The door to the outbuilding was open, and she saw that this end of it had once been a chicken coop, judging by the nesting boxes. Bear whined and tugged, but she kept him firmly under control.

The interior still held the aroma of hay and dust and, just faintly, a remnant of chickens. Kaylee stepped inside. "Boyd?" she called. "Are you in here?"

Nothing. She called again. Then she heard a faint groan. "Help. Someone help me."

9

Kaylee bolted through the chicken coop, Bear whining and pulling on the leash. In the doorway to another room, she tripped over something and almost fell flat. By some miracle, she managed to catch herself against a stall wall. In the process, she let go of the leash and Bear darted into the darkness.

She reached down and grabbed the thing she'd tripped on. It was a short shovel with a handle. She tossed it aside and kept going.

Boyd lay on the floor in the third room, which was full of old farm junk and lit only by a tiny window high in the wall. Kaylee spotted an open trapdoor in the floor and a light shining up from down below.

Bear was nudging Boyd's shoulder, alternating with licking his cheek. "Bear, stop." Kaylee set her pet aside and crouched beside the writer. "Boyd. Talk to me."

He put a hand over his face, groaning again. "Someone hit me. I almost fell into the hole."

"Did you see who it was?" Kaylee used the light function on her phone to check him over.

"No." He groaned again and shut his eyes. "My head hurts."

Her belly flipped over when she saw blood matting his hair. "I'm calling an ambulance." With shaking fingers, she dialed 911.

The dispatcher promised that an ambulance and the police would be there quickly. But in such a remote location, Kaylee knew it would take a few minutes. "They'll be here soon," she told the injured man, hoping she sounded calm and reassuring.

This time, Boyd didn't respond. Using her light, she saw that he was unconscious. He didn't react when she shook him, and now she prayed the ambulance would hurry. It was chilly in the shed, and she thought about taking off her jacket and covering him. But what if there was some kind of evidence on his clothing or skin? She didn't want to interfere with that. It was bad enough they would find dog slobber and hair on him.

Bear was watching her from the shadows with his big eyes. He whined and pawed at the wooden floor, as though wanting to run.

"You're a good boy, Bear," she said. "Come here."

He trotted toward her, careful to skirt the hole in the floor. After grabbing the leash, Kaylee edged closer to the opening, keeping one eye on Boyd to make sure his chest still rose and fell.

A battery-powered lantern lay on the dirt floor below with a pickax beside it, and Kaylee guessed Boyd must have dropped those. From the animal odors wafting up, it appeared the cellar had once been a hatch for manure disposal. She'd seen similar arrangements at other farms. Usually there was another way to get the waste outside the building. Perhaps that had been boarded up or blocked. Otherwise, surely Boyd would have gone in that route.

She'd answered the question of what Boyd had been doing. The larger issue was who had struck him down? The memory of seeing Kathy in her car drifted through her mind, immediately followed by revulsion and disbelief. Surely Kathy hadn't attacked her ex-husband after cozying up to him for the past several days.

The welcome siren of the ambulance arriving split the foggy air. Kaylee realized the EMTs might not be able to find them right off, so she walked across the field, waving her arms and calling out.

Violet Moore appeared at the edge of the orchard. She hesitated when she saw Kaylee. "What's going on?"

"Boyd is hurt." Kaylee bit off any further explanation. She didn't want to taint the case for the police and although she'd love to ask Violet questions, she refrained.

The farmer's wife gasped. "What happened?" She looked around as if hoping to spot the injured writer.

"I'm not sure," Kaylee said. "Excuse me." She continued walking across the field to the ambulance. A county sheriff's cruiser pulled in, jerking to a stop next to the ambulance. Robyn Garcia and Alan Brooks climbed out, both appearing surprised to see Kaylee.

"I came out here a short while ago to bring Boyd some research material," she told them. "I found him suffering from a head injury in one of the outbuildings."

The EMTs had pulled a stretcher from the rear of the ambulance. "Where to, ma'am?" one asked.

"I'll show you." Kaylee led the way, noticing that Violet was still lurking among the apple trees.

Deputy Brooks saw her too. "Stay back please, Mrs. Moore. We'll talk to you later."

So the police were acquainted with Violet. Kaylee filed that away, but realized it could mean nothing. After all, she practically had them on speed dial, and she was one of the good guys.

Once she showed the way to Boyd in the chicken coop, she stayed outside with Bear, allowing the medical and law enforcement personnel to do their jobs. After a few minutes, Deputy Brooks joined her.

"Want to take me through what happened?" he asked, poised to take notes on his tablet.

She gave him a detailed description of her morning, including the approximate times she'd left her house and found Boyd.

"Did you see anyone else on the property?" he asked. "Or leaving, by chance?"

Kathy Fitz came to mind. She hadn't been near Buttercup Cottage but certainly in the vicinity. As Kaylee opened her mouth to tell him that—with no small amount of reluctance—Deputy Garcia appeared in the doorway. "Alan, I think we found the weapon."

"Hold that thought, Kaylee," he said.

He rushed toward Deputy Garcia, and as they went farther into the building, Kaylee heard Robyn say, "I found a shovel with blood on the blade."

A shovel with blood? Kaylee swayed, suddenly woozy. Were they talking about the shovel she had picked up and thrown aside?

"What's the matter?" Violet asked, appearing at Kaylee's side. "Are you okay?"

Kaylee sucked in a deep breath. "I'm fine." She heard the sound of voices from inside. "We'd better get out of the way so the EMTs can get through." Trembling, she moved away from the doorway.

Boyd was still unconscious, an oxygen mask over his nose. Violet gave a little scream and approached the stretcher. "What happened to him? Is he going to be all right?"

"I can't discuss that with you," one of the EMTs said. He and the other man worked together to coordinate Boyd's transport to the ambulance. Within a short time, they had loaded him inside and they sped off, the siren wailing.

The police were still working inside and Kaylee stood irresolute, wondering how long she would have to stay.

Deputy Brooks finally emerged again. "Kaylee, I have a few more questions. Then you can go, as long as I can reach you."

"I'll be at the shop and, of course, near my cell phone." Kaylee gulped. "Um, I couldn't help but overhear you say something about a shovel. I tripped over one when I went in there and tossed it aside. It was in my way."

His gaze sharpened and although his movements were barely discernible, Kaylee had the impression that every sense was on alert. He described the shovel. "Does that sound like the one you picked up?"

Kaylee nodded glumly. She had touched the assault weapon, perhaps obliterating the attacker's fingerprints. "I guess you'll want my prints for elimination purposes."

Violet was all ears. "You mean Boyd was attacked? That's awful!" She shivered, glancing over her shoulder fearfully. "Who would do such a thing?"

"I don't know, Mrs. Moore," Deputy Brooks said. "Got any ideas?"

Hunching her shoulders, Violet bit her lip and shook her head.

The deputy studied her for a long moment. "I'll talk to you in a minute, if you'll excuse us." Once Violet had walked away, he said, "Kaylee, I'm going to let you go for now. Later this morning, come down to the station and we'll do a fresh set of your prints. If you think of anything that might be important, let me know."

"I'll do that." Kaylee picked up Bear's leash. Then she thought of something she needed to know. "Is Boyd going to be all right?"

"Yes, as far as we can tell. You getting here when you did made a big difference. You might have saved his life."

Kaylee took a deep, anxious breath. She had to mention Kathy. "There is one more thing. On the way here, I saw Kathy Fitz, the librarian, coming the other way, from this direction." She squirmed with discomfort at pointing a finger at a friend. "I don't know for sure if she was here or anything, but she and Boyd have been seeing each other. I can't imagine her doing something like this, though," she added firmly.

The deputy seemed not to hear the last comment. "She's his ex-wife, right?" He made a note. "Thanks for passing that along, Kaylee."

Feeling like a traitor, Kaylee took Bear back to the car and headed for Turtle Cove.

When she reached the shop, Kaylee decided she needed a treat from Death by Chocolate. Since Bear wasn't allowed inside the bakery, she let him into The Flower Patch with a promise that she'd be back soon. She was locking the door again when two men came down the sidewalk.

"I heard you found a body yesterday," one asked.

Kaylee swiveled and found herself face-to-face with the bird-watchers. "Not exactly," she said with a laugh. "More of a skeleton."

"Did you find the treasure too?" the short, stout one asked. He rubbed his hands together. "That would be something."

"No, we didn't find the treasure." Kaylee waved at Bear, who had his face pressed to the display window.

"That your dog?" the taller one asked. "What breed is that?"

"He's a dachshund," Kaylee explained. She started to stroll down the sidewalk toward Death by Chocolate, hoping the men would get the hint and move on. But to her chagrin, they accompanied her down the sidewalk.

"They bark too much," the short one said. "I don't like yappy dogs."

Kaylee had reached Death by Chocolate and now she reached for the door handle, swallowing her anger. "Have a nice day, guys. See you later." She popped inside, hoping they wouldn't follow.

Jessica was working behind the counter. "What's new, Kaylee?" she asked, arranging some fresh-baked éclairs.

Kaylee didn't know where to begin, so she focused on the pastries. "Those look spectacular."

"The éclair is making a comeback," the baker said. "I've got strawberry chocolate, caramel dark chocolate, and cherry chocolate."

Kaylee couldn't resist. "Strawberry chocolate, please. And a large coffee to go."

The bells over the door jangled and Kathy walked inside. Kaylee cringed, not ready to confront the librarian. What if she'd learned that Kaylee had reported her to the deputy?

"Hey, Kaylee," Kathy said, appearing at her elbow. "Was that you I saw this morning driving out toward Madrona Grove?" She bent to study the contents of the bakery case.

"Yes, that was me." Kaylee's heart began to pound as she tensed for an argument. "I was taking Edna's papers over to Boyd's."

"Oh, how was he?" Kathy pointed at Kaylee's éclair. "That smells amazing. I want one of those."

Doesn't she know? Kaylee felt her mouth drop open. How was she going to tell Kathy that Boyd was hurt and that she was a suspect?

Kathy's phone rang and she pulled it out of a side pocket in her handbag. She peered at the name on the display and frowned. "The sheriff's department? What do they want?" She stepped aside to take the call.

Jessica brought Kaylee's coffee to the counter. "Here you go." She rang up the sale. Kaylee paid automatically, her attention on the phone conversation taking place a few feet away.

Kathy gave a little shriek. "What do you mean, he's hurt? Of course I don't know anything about it." She listened. "I'll be right there."

"What's going on?" Jessica's gaze followed Kaylee's to Kathy. Kaylee could imagine all too well. "I'll tell you later, okay?"

The librarian dropped her phone into her purse and approached the counter. "Sorry, Jessica, I have to cancel my order. I've been summoned to the sheriff's department." Her voice rose with emotion. "Boyd was attacked, and they think I did it."

10

Kathy pivoted on her heel and ran from the bakery. Kaylee set her cup and paper bag on the counter. "I'm going after her."

"Will somebody please tell me what's happening?" Jessica called.

Without answering, Kaylee pulled the bakery door open and raced down the steps. Kathy was striding toward her car, keys held at the ready. Tears streamed down her face. Guilt twisted in Kaylee's stomach. "Kathy, wait."

"What?" Kathy halted but didn't face Kaylee. "I need to get to the sheriff's department."

Kaylee swallowed. "I was the one who told them you were nearby." She winced. "I had to."

"You what?" The librarian whirled around, emotions ranging from despair to anger flashing across her face. She stamped her foot indignantly. "For your information, I wasn't at Boyd's this morning. I drove over to talk to him but chickened out before I got there."

"About what?" Kaylee's hand flew to her mouth. *None of your business.*

"If you must know, I wanted to talk about our future. We've been getting along great, better than ever. Now the sheriff thinks I attacked him."

"Did they actually tell you that?"

"No, but why else would they want to talk to me?" Kathy released an aggravated sigh, then turned around and pushed the unlock button, fumbling a couple of times. Finally, the car beeped and she pulled the door open with shaking hands. She jumped inside and slammed the door, then started the engine and roared away.

Kaylee stood on the curb, watching the little blue car until it was out of sight. What else could she have done? She sighed and returned to the bakery. If Kathy was telling the truth, then it would be okay. And maybe she'd forgive Kaylee.

Inside Death by Chocolate, Jessica stared at her with big eyes. "Will you please fill me in? I'm dying here."

Kaylee glanced around at the crowded room. "Can we talk somewhere a little more private?" She picked up her coffee and took a sip, soaking in its warmth.

The baker gestured to Jenny, one of her employees. "Can you please take over for a minute? Thanks." Jessica came around the counter. "Let's go to my office."

Jessica's office was a cubbyhole in the back with room only for a desk, file cabinet, and two chairs. Still holding her coffee, Kaylee squeezed into the visitor chair while Jessica plopped down behind the desk. She picked up a pile of folders and put them aside with a laugh. "Paperwork never ends." She rested her chin on her propped hands. "So spill."

"Where to begin? Do you want finding the skeleton or Boyd being hit over the head?"

Jessica pushed back in her chair with a squeal that was echoed by her ancient chair. "Kaylee! You've been holding out on me." She rolled back to the desk. "Start at the beginning."

Kaylee took her through the events of the previous day, the trip to Blossom Island and the discovery of Jack Butler's skeleton. Then she explained how she'd driven out to Buttercup Cottage that morning and found Boyd injured. "I had to tell Deputy Brooks about seeing Kathy. I understand her reaction, of course." Kaylee shook her head. "I wouldn't want to be suspected of assaulting the man I love."

"She still loves him?" It was so like Jessica to focus in on that. "Oh my. That is not good." Her dark brows drew together in a scowl. "I'm going to have to talk to that woman. She's usually so levelheaded, but when it comes to Boyd—"

"Maybe they'll reconcile," Kaylee said. "It might be really romantic."

Jessica wagged a finger. "Boyd Parsons is devilishly handsome and charming, I'll give him that. But if this was the 1800s, he'd be called a rake." She tapped that finger on her chin. "Or a cad. Or a louse, maybe."

"I get it." Kaylee sighed. "Guess what? I touched the weapon, so I have to go to the sheriff's office too." She explained how she had stumbled over the shovel.

Jessica shuddered. "Gruesome. I'm glad Boyd is going to be okay, even if he is a rat."

Kaylee arrived at a quiet sheriff's department later that morning. From where she perched in the waiting room, she could hear phones ringing but nothing else. Even Aida Friedman, the usually talkative receptionist, was working intently at her computer, rolling back and forth as she grabbed files.

The table beside Kaylee held only ancient copies of fishing magazines so she contented herself with reading the *Wanted* posters. As she studied each face, reading the list of crimes they'd allegedly committed, Kaylee wondered about Jack Butler and Lester Clayton. Had posters been created for them? It would be interesting to dig into the history of the bank robbers, especially since Edna Taylor had once worked in her building. She still had Edna's crate in her car. Hopefully Boyd would be well enough to go through it soon.

A door opened. "Kaylee? We're ready for you." Deputy Brooks stood in the doorway to the back, his hand on the knob. "Sorry to make you do this when we already have an ink set on file, but we just upgraded our computer system and it's better to get a fresh set electronically."

Kaylee nodded and followed, her pulse leaping up a notch. Even though she was innocent of any wrongdoing, getting her fingerprints taken still felt a little frightening.

While Deputy Brooks watched, another deputy performed the task of electronically recording Kaylee's fingers. After she was finished, Deputy Brooks said, "That's all for today, unless you've remembered something else."

"Not yet," Kaylee said.

Deputy Brooks escorted Kaylee toward the door. "Your tip helped a great deal." He lowered his voice. "We made an arrest. The press release is coming out this afternoon."

Cold shock and dismay flooded Kaylee. She had a bad feeling about the direction this was going. "Already?"

He nodded, his lips pressed together into a grim line. "The suspect used her own shovel. Crime of passion, no doubt."

In a daze, Kaylee wandered out of the station and made her way back to the shop. She couldn't help but feel responsible for Kathy's arrest, although the news that the weapon was the librarian's shovel surprised her. Her fertile imagination could picture all too well Kathy bringing the shovel over for Boyd to use. Then something triggered a fit of anger and bam—she hit him, dropped the shovel, and ran.

But he claimed not to have seen his assailant. Was he lying to protect Kathy after a lover's spat?

The whole thing was sickening, especially since she genuinely liked Kathy and certainly had never seen any indications of a fiery temper.

"How did it go?" Mary asked when Kaylee entered The Flower Patch. She continued to press a round sponge dauber onto a miniature pumpkin, creating pea-size white polka dots.

"Cute design," Kaylee said. She set her handbag behind the counter and bent down to greet Bear. "Kathy Fitz was arrested for assaulting Boyd." She'd already filled in her assistant regarding the events of the last two days. "Apparently it was her shovel that was used to hit him."

Mary gave a little squeal of shock. She set down the painting tool and put a hand to her chest. "No. I refuse to believe that." Her lips curved in a grim smile. "The time for assault was twenty years ago, when he left her. Not now, when even the embers are long cold."

Kaylee gave Bear a final pat and stood, groaning a little. "Unless the flames have been rekindled. The two of them have been quite friendly when I've seen them together." She leaned against the counter and crossed her arms. "I feel treacherous even saying that. I consider Kathy a friend."

Mary picked up the dauber again. "Remember, she's innocent until proven guilty. Maybe her shovel was already there and the assailant happened to grab it."

Kaylee's gloom lifted a little. "You could be right. Perhaps we can figure out who did it." She smiled at Mary. "Put me to work. I need to get my mind off this situation and do something useful."

"We have tons to do, so no problem." Mary handed her a dauber and a bottle of gold paint, then pointed to a fresh white pumpkin. "Make polka dots on this pumpkin."

The front doorbells jingled and DeeDee stepped inside. "Have you heard the news? Kathy Fitz was arrested." She waved her phone. "I just saw it on social media."

Mary and Kaylee exchanged glances. "Yes, we know," Kaylee

said. "And I'm the one responsible." Taking a deep breath, she told DeeDee everything she knew.

"I can't believe Kathy would do it," DeeDee said firmly. "Of course I never thought she'd give Boyd another chance either. Even though he is a dreamboat." She laughed. "Sorry. I was playing a vintage dating board game with the girls last night."

"I remember that game," Mary said. "As for Kathy, I agree that she's innocent. I've never seen her lose her temper, not once in the twenty years I've known her. That would be so out of character."

Kaylee turned the pumpkin and added additional dots. "What do you think of these pumpkins, DeeDee?"

DeeDee moved closer to the counter. "They're adorable. Can you make white ones with pink dots?"

"I don't see why not," Mary said. "All we need is pink paint and white pumpkins."

"I'll take thirty miniature ones for Zoe's scout troop." DeeDee grinned. "They'll get such a kick out of them." She fingered some pink ribbon on the rack. "Maybe tie ribbons around them too?"

"We can do that." Mary nodded at Kaylee. "We'll need to buy more from the farm."

"I'd better get back to the store," DeeDee said. But she lingered. "How was it finding that skeleton?"

"Fortunately, all I saw was a belt buckle and a pocket watch," Kaylee said. "The rest of it, no thanks."

"I hear you. I prefer my skeletons in stories, not real life." On her way to the door, DeeDee halted. "Oh, I forgot why I came in here. Are you all set for Anything But Pie? Jess asked me to check with all the businesses."

Kaylee smiled. "I sure am. I found a recipe for pumpkin macarons."

"Macarons?" DeeDee raised an eyebrow. "Are you sure you're up for the challenge? They're pretty advanced."

Kaylee shrugged. "I used to make them with Grandma, and I think I remember some tricks. How hard can they be?"

"I'll make something extra in case they don't work out," Mary said. At Kaylee's glance, she raised both hands. "What? I gave up on macarons years ago."

"On that note, I'm out of here." DeeDee opened the door. "See you later."

Kaylee bit her tongue. She'd found what she thought was a foolproof recipe and she wouldn't say another word. They'd all be surprised at the bake sale when she showed up with perfect, light-as-air cookies.

Mary picked up the shop telephone. "Let me check with the farm and see if they still have enough pumpkins for DeeDee's order." She placed the call and ordered an extra twenty on top of the thirty for DeeDee. "They're open every day this week until four," she told Kaylee when she hung up.

Kaylee checked the time, a tempting thought percolating in her brain. It was probably a really bad idea, but once she'd formulated it, she had trouble letting go. "I'll drive over now, if that's okay with you," she offered. At the word *drive*, Bear jumped down from his chair and began wagging his tail.

Mary glanced through the daily order list attached to a clipboard. "We're all caught up, so that should be fine. See you back here before we close?"

"I don't see why not." Kaylee jingled her keys, a move that made Bear prance excitedly, his nails clicking on the hardwood floor. "The fog cleared up so it should be a quick trip."

It was fortunate that Kaylee was now familiar with the route to Madrona Grove Road, because she spent the entire time debating with herself. The closer she got to her destination, the more strongly her tempting idea called to her. And when she saw the farm sign, she found herself stepping on the gas and zooming past the entrance.

She was going to check Buttercup Cottage for clues while she had the chance.

Bear whined when she turned into the property, seeming to know where he was going. "Boyd's not here, Bear," she said. "But we're going to take a little walk around."

The dog began to bounce up and down on the car seat, yipping eagerly. Next to *drive, walk* was his favorite word. He pressed his nose against the glass, watching the trees as she drove slowly into the yard. She wasn't sure what she would do if the deputies were there.

The parking area was empty, and Buttercup Cottage seemed at peace in the afternoon sun. Late crickets chirped in the long grass as Kaylee and Bear got out of the car. She clipped on his leash and strolled toward the outbuildings. With their fixation on Kathy, had the deputies searched for evidence as thoroughly as they might?

She made a circuit of the cottage first, checking near the two entrances and around the building. The grass was short and the bushes trimmed back from the windows. Nothing obvious jumped out at her. There were no footprints in the flower bed or pieces of paper dropped from a pocket.

A short distance away, Bear was sniffing the ground intently, resistant when she tugged. "What is it, Bear?" She hoped he hadn't discovered something distasteful.

Bear had his nose in a little pile of sunflower seed hulls sitting under a hydrangea bush heavy with flowers drying into beige poofs. Kaylee looked from the seed pile to the house. There was a direct line of sight right into the kitchen. Unless Boyd enjoyed standing out here in the yard or a workman had left them, it was possible a snoop had watched him from here. *Interesting.*

Kaylee walked the rest of the way around the house, scouting for sunflower seeds. She found another sprinkle in the field, near where the grass was compressed by people walking through. This was the path Violet had used to come over from the farm, where they sold sunflower seeds. Had she been spying on her former boyfriend?

Intrigued, Kaylee followed the trail into the woods. Here, the grass became dirt, leaves, and pine needles. Right inside the line of the trees, she found more sunflower seed hulls. From here, she could see the whole of Buttercup Cottage and the driveway.

In the depths of the forest, something cracked with a loud snap. Bear went on high alert, his nose raised as he sniffed.

"It's probably just a squirrel, Bear." Kaylee peered into the underbrush, but was unable to discern any movement.

Shrugging, she turned back to the seed hulls. What should she do? These shells might be evidence, or they might mean absolutely nothing. She crouched down to examine them more closely, thinking. If she collected them, they couldn't be used to build a case. On the other hand, dragging deputies out here to look at sunflower seeds would be ludicrous.

Kaylee pulled out her phone and took a photo. Foraging in her pocket, she found a tissue and wrapped a small sample in it. Then she grabbed a nearby rock and placed it carefully over the hulls. They would decay eventually, but this would do for now. She'd do the same for the ones next to the house. The location of both piles spoke to a watcher, not a casual walker shedding shells as they strolled.

Another branch snapped nearby, making Kaylee lose her balance as she crouched over the seed hulls. She found herself sitting in the dirt.

Bear began to bark and pull at the leash, every muscle in his body tense.

Kaylee peered into the trees—and gasped.

Someone was watching her.

11

The figure stood unmoving in the shadows, a ball cap pulled low to hide any identifying features. Kaylee pushed herself to her feet, chills of panic running through her limbs. Was that the person who attacked Boyd? The driver of the truck who hit her car?

"Come on, Bear, we're getting out of here." Kaylee scooped up the little dog and ran down the path toward the field, the sun's weak warmth beckoning like an oasis. She was winded halfway through, but she continued to run, not stopping until she reached her Escape. She jumped inside with Bear, locked the doors, and started the engine.

As she backed the car and drove forward, Bear growled and gave a couple of yaps. She didn't bother to glance behind to see if the person had pursued her. She raced down the driveway, scattering gravel.

Once on Madrona Grove Road, she was tempted to continue on toward town, but she slowed to turn into the farm instead. She needed to get those pumpkins for the shop. But if she spotted a figure wearing a ball cap, she was not getting out of the car unless someone else was around.

The dooryard of the farm was empty of both customers and lurking strangers. As Kaylee parked near the barn, she saw a scowling Violet emerge from the house lugging a duffel bag. She carried it to a small red sedan, opened the hatch, and threw it in. Then she noticed Kaylee and gave an unsmiling nod.

Kaylee opened her door and got out. "Good morning, Violet. I'm here to pick up an order of pumpkins for The Flower Patch."

Violet pointed to a crate sitting beside the barn's open doors. "They're over there, along with an invoice," she said coldly. "You can pay us—Paul—later." She turned and trotted up the steps into the house.

What's up with her? Confused by the farmer's surly attitude, Kaylee went to get the crate. By the time she examined the invoice to be sure she had the right number of pumpkins, Violet was outside again, this time with several small bags that she threw into the backseat.

"I think I'm all set," Kaylee called.

"Good, 'cause I'm out of here." The other woman went around to the driver's side. She hopped into her car, adjusted the mirror, and started the engine.

Shaking her head, Kaylee picked up the box of pumpkins and carried it to the car. She was as eager to depart as Violet had been. Was she leaving her husband? It sure looked that way. People going on vacation were usually happy. Violet had seemed anything but.

On the way back to town, Kaylee's phone trilled. She never spoke on the phone while driving but she did spare the screen a glance. It was Kathy Fitz. Kaylee pulled over and took the call.

"Hi, Kathy. How are you?" Kaylee didn't want to let on that she knew about the arrest, although she had heard that Kathy was already released on bail.

Kathy sniffed. "I was arrested for allegedly assaulting my former husband. And I've been forced into a leave of absence by the library trustees to boot. How would you be doing?"

"I'm sorry, Kathy." Kaylee kept her voice mild, trying to hide her emotions. "How can I help you?" Her heart twisted with pity for the woman. Orcas Island was a small community and unless Kathy was cleared, her livelihood was in peril.

"Can you pick up Boyd at the hospital tomorrow at noon?

One condition of my release is that I can't go anywhere near him." She began to cry. "It's so unfair. Just because he had my shovel there, which naturally had my prints, they're blaming me."

Guilt twisted once again. Kaylee knew that her sighting of Kathy nearby was a key piece in the sheriff's case. Was Kathy telling the truth and she really hadn't seen Boyd that morning? But if not, had she witnessed something important without realizing it? A spark of energy ran through Kaylee's veins. "Did you see anyone on your way out there? Someone else who might have done it?"

"Who would want to hurt Boyd?" Kathy's tone was glum. "He's a great guy."

Kaylee recalled a story she'd heard during a Petal Pushers meeting. It was a stretch but just maybe a valid theory. "I like him too. But think about it—he's put away some criminals, right? It could be that one of them wanted revenge." Which could mean Boyd was still in danger.

"Maybe." Kathy's tone lost a touch of its gloom. "We could ask him. And there's always the issue of former girlfriends. I don't hold a grudge, but one of them might."

"Like Violet?" The words popped out of Kaylee's mouth. "I shouldn't have said that." She certainly didn't want to spread rumors that would hurt a married woman's reputation.

Kathy snorted. "Violet. She's been hanging around a lot since Boyd got back. Not a good idea. Paul is a great guy, but he's also the jealous type."

"You think she still has feelings for Boyd?" Kaylee felt a pang of remorse for continuing the conversation in this vein. But she couldn't resist trying to find out whatever Kathy could tell her. It might explain Violet's hasty exit from the farm.

"What can I tell you? Boyd's the type of guy you never get over." Kathy sighed. "Being with him is magical. There's no other word for it."

Kaylee wasn't quite sure how to respond to that so she merely said, "I'll pick up Boyd tomorrow." She paused. "And hang in there, Kathy. We'll figure this out."

As she drove on, she hoped fervently she hadn't made a promise she couldn't keep.

That evening, the temperature plunged, so Kaylee made a fire in the fireplace after a dinner of leftover shepherd's pie. As the enticing aroma of burning applewood filled the air, she took a deep breath of satisfaction. While she loved summer, there was something inherently wonderful about a cozy fire on a cold night.

"Let's do a little research tonight, Bear," she said. Seated on a nearby armchair, the dachshund cocked his head in inquiry. "I'm thinking we'll go through Edna's papers." Bear yawned and Kaylee laughed. "Now, you don't know it'll be boring. We might find something interesting in there that'll crack the whole case."

She felt a tickle of excitement when she brought the crate in from the car and set it on the hearthrug. She'd developed a flair for research during her academic career and loved ferreting out interesting nuggets in unlikely places. Making connections between disparate pieces of information was another talent she'd honed. These skills, plus a healthy dose of patience, helped a great deal when trying to solve the mysteries that kept finding her.

Kaylee made a fresh cup of tea, then sat cross-legged on the rug to look through the crate. The scent of musty papers met her nose as she removed the top. At first glance, the contents were a jumble, most of the paper itself yellowed and faded.

She reached inside and pulled out the first item. It was a bill for bolts of fabric—cotton, crepe, voile, and dimity. She put it aside, deciding to make piles of like items. The sorting went fairly quickly. She found dozens of preprinted patterns, a customer ledger, more bills and invoices, a few photographs, and letters, both personal and business.

Most of the materials would be of interest to someone researching dressmaking or small businesses in the 1930s. Kaylee glanced through the photos first. They showed Edna in front of Buttercup Cottage, at her sewing machine, and in her shop. She studied that one closely, curious to see what the space had looked like back then. One thing she noticed were the curtains—diamond-patterned brocade tied back with swags. The woodwork was the same and, Kaylee was pleased to see, the shop still had the original counter.

Next she turned to the letters, which she'd sorted by sender, and started reading through the business correspondence. Edna had once had a substantial sum of money in a Seattle bank, she learned, and a quick online search confirmed Kaylee's suspicion. It was the same bank Lester and his cohorts had robbed.

She opened those envelopes, finding a few statements and then an interesting letter verifying that Edna had closed her account. The date was one week before the robbery.

Interesting timing. Did Edna have foreknowledge of the crime, tipped off by Lester? Kaylee studied the letter again, noting the name of the bank president, Orville Clayton. *The same last name as Lester.* Again, very interesting. Clayton wasn't the most unusual name, but still it was worth investigating a connection.

Kaylee set the bank letters aside to show Boyd. The dress patterns she stacked on a shelf for one of Mary's friends who loved to sew. Then she refreshed her cup of tea and opened the first personal letter.

She didn't find any written by Lester, unfortunately, so there was no proof of a prior relationship. One letter had a return address of Maisie Fitz, from Eastsound. *Fitz.* Was this a relative of Kathy's? She had returned to her maiden name after her divorce.

Inside the envelope were a couple of folded sheets and at the top of the first was a date a few weeks before the bank robbery.

> *Dearest friend,*
>
> *I can't believe I haven't made it down to Turtle Cove to see your new shop. I do need a dress or two, so I'll have to make that a priority. I've been so busy running the farm while Albert is away fishing. That and five children will keep a body busy!*

The letter went on about Maisie's life for a couple of paragraphs, then it was back to Edna.

> *How is your aunt Harriet doing? I've been praying for her since I learned that her son was injured and is laid up. Tell her I'll send my hired hand down if she needs help. It's the least I can do to help the Moores, as they've been both good family and good neighbors to you.*

Harriet Moore? Maisie must be talking about Paul Moore's grandmother or great-grandmother. Maybe he'd like to see this letter. Kathy too. Kaylee filed that thought and kept reading.

As for you, my dear, when are we going to meet this mystery man of yours? All you've told me is that you met in Seattle when you were there on business. You don't need to be shy with me. I'm happy for you. You've been alone long enough.

A thrill of discovery quickened Kaylee's heartbeat. Between the bank statements and this letter, it sure seemed Edna Taylor had been involved with Lester Clayton and maybe even the bank robbery. It was a place for Boyd to start, anyway.

At a few minutes to noon the next day, Kaylee pulled into the hospital parking lot. Since she was picking up a patient, she parked close to the double doors, with a plan to pull around when Boyd was rolled outside.

Inside the lobby, she approached the information desk, where a staff person gave her directions to the elevator. Boyd's room was on the second floor. She shared the elevator with a man carrying a teddy bear and several pink balloons. By his nervous and excited face—and the message on the balloons—she guessed he was a new father.

"Congratulations," she said. "What's her name?"

A grin burst over his face. "Ava Willow. Seven pounds, six ounces." He tucked the teddy bear under the other arm and ran a hand over his thick, dark hair. "She has my hair and her mama's eyes."

"She must be beautiful." Although Kaylee didn't have children of her own, she adored them, especially her two nieces in Florida.

"She is," he said proudly.

The maternity ward was also on the second floor, but in the opposite direction. Sharing a final smile, Kaylee and her companion went their separate ways.

A nurse directed Kaylee to the right room and as she approached, she heard two voices. Worried that Boyd might be in the middle of an examination, she hesitated outside the open door.

"Are you sure you don't remember seeing someone?" That voice was familiar.

Kaylee peeked around the corner. Violet was leaning against the wall with arms crossed, talking to Boyd, who was seated in a chair.

"I don't remember a thing." He shook his bandaged head, then put a hand to his temple with a wince. "I've got to stop doing that. No, I was working in my shed when someone or something hit me, and wham—lights out."

"They arrested Kathy, you know." Violet's tone was abrupt. "Her fingerprints were all over the shovel that she whacked you with."

"Of course her fingerprints were all over it. It's her shovel. She lent it to me. It could have been anyone who attacked me."

Violet pushed herself away from the wall, her eyes wide. "But who? No one else has a reason to hurt you." Her voice trembled slightly and she bit her lip.

"And does Kathy?" Boyd cocked his head and gave her a strange half-smile. "Why, Violet. Do you know something I don't? Fill me in."

Kaylee thought the same thing—that Violet suspected someone. Was it her jealous husband? Or was she the culprit?

Violet ran both hands through her hair, pushing it away from her face. "Of course not. I'm just saying that Kathy is the logical one, that's all."

Boyd snorted. "Innocent until proven guilty. I'm not exactly popular back on the mainland either, you know."

Kaylee heard the squeak of nurses' shoes coming along the hallway. Not wanting to be caught eavesdropping, she knocked on the doorjamb and walked inside. "Good afternoon, Boyd. I'm here to take you home."

"You're taking him?" Violet frowned. "I thought I would do that."

"It's all been arranged," Kaylee said. "Unless you want to change your mind, Boyd." She shrugged. "All the same to me."

Boyd pushed himself to a standing position, moving slowly as if he felt fragile. "I'll go with you, Kaylee. I really appreciate you making the time." He faced Violet when she huffed. "It's not true, Violet, so put it out of your mind."

"I guess I know when I'm not wanted. See you later." The other woman whirled around and stomped out of the room, pushing rudely past the nurse entering.

"My, my," the nurse said. "Another one of your fans, Mr. Parsons?" Her teasing tone said that she knew he had plenty.

"Not anymore," Boyd said. "Are you here to spring me out of this joint?"

"Yes, sir, long as you behave yourself." She looked at Kaylee. "I'm assuming you're his ride?"

"I am. Kaylee Bleu." While the nurse checked the paperwork, Kaylee smiled at Boyd. "Do you want something to eat or drink?" she asked. "I can pop into the cafeteria. I'm thinking of grabbing a sandwich."

"I wouldn't say no to bottled water and a sandwich," Boyd said.

"Do I have time to run down?" Kaylee asked the nurse.

"Sure thing. We'll wait for you in the lobby."

Kaylee took the elevator back to the first floor and followed the signs to the cafeteria. Once inside, she grabbed two bottles of water then joined the line edging along the sandwich section.

"Hello again," a voice said from behind her.

She turned to see the two bird-watchers sitting at a table eating lunch off trays. "Good afternoon. How are you?"

The stout one pointed at his friend. "Pretty good until Ned scraped his hand on a rusty nail." He ate the last spoonful of soup from his bowl.

"Had to get a tetanus booster." Ned held up the injured hand, which was wrapped in a bandage. "Who actually gets them as scheduled?" He chuckled. "I sure don't."

"Where did you run into a rusty nail?" Kaylee asked. "Not where you're staying, surely."

The men eyed each other, then the stout one said, "At that farm. All kinds of rusty metal around that place." He checked his friend's tray. "You about ready to get out of here?"

People waiting behind Kaylee were getting impatient, and she noticed she'd allowed a large space to form between herself and the people ahead of her. "Oops. I'd better go. Hope you have a good day. Or at least a better one."

By the time Kaylee bought two sandwiches, chips, and the water, the bird-watchers were gone. She went to meet Boyd and the nurse in the lobby.

Boyd looked relieved when she appeared. "I thought maybe you'd changed your mind."

"Of course not," Kaylee said. "A lot of other people were getting lunch too."

The nurse pushed Boyd outside through the automatic doors.

"This is so ridiculous," Boyd said. "I can walk from here."

The nurse patted his broad shoulder. "I know that, but it's policy. Wheel you in, wheel you out."

Kaylee pulled her Escape out of its spot and parked by the

curb so the nurse could help Boyd inside. "Be sure to buckle up now," the nurse said. "We don't want to see you back here."

"Yes, ma'am." Boyd gave her his heartbreaking grin. "Thank you for all your help."

Blushing, the nurse hurried back inside the hospital. As Kaylee pulled ahead, she spotted a familiar face across the parking lot. Kathy was standing next to her car, staring their way. "Kathy is here," Kaylee said to Boyd. "She's probably breaking the terms of her arrest."

"I won't tell," Boyd said. He gave Kathy a wave. "Who are those men talking to her? Do you know them by chance?"

Kaylee glanced over as she slowly drove through the lot. The bird-watchers were standing near Kathy, who was gesturing and saying something. "They're tourists staying in town. Probably asking her for directions."

As she continued along the lane to the exit, Boyd stared back over his shoulder, a frown creasing his brow. "I don't like the looks of those guys," he muttered. "Not a bit."

12

On the drive to Buttercup Cottage, conversation didn't land on the bank robbery or Boyd's relationship with Kathy. Instead, Boyd asked Kaylee a more ominous question.

"Do you know someone who can install a security system?" Boyd asked. "I want to put one in at the cottage."

"Are you worried about your assailant coming back?" Kaylee thought of the person watching her in the woods and shivered. Was that the person who attacked Boyd?

The writer studied the passing scenery. "It's more that I don't want people snooping around. If there's something important on the property, I want to be the one to find it."

"That's a good idea, actually. A lot of people go through your land," Kaylee said. "There's quite a beaten path between your cottage and the farm. And I saw someone in the woods the other day." She hoped he wouldn't ask exactly when, since she'd been poking around without permission at the time.

Boyd didn't seem concerned. "There's conservation land all around my property and the farm. It's accessed by walkers, bird-watchers, all kinds of people. I saw a scout troop crashing around in the woods one day."

Remembering the seeds, Kaylee said, "You might want to consider putting up Private Property signs, because they also trespass. I found heaps of sunflower seed hulls right next to your house. Unless they were yours?"

"Not mine." He gave her a funny look. "You take this investigating thing seriously, don't you? Not many people would have noticed those."

Kaylee squirmed. "What can I say? I have an eye for detail."

"Probably one of the workmen I hired to fix a few things around the place dropped them." Boyd shrugged. "They certainly left enough wood and sawdust debris."

He could be right. But she asked anyway, "When were they there?"

"A few weeks ago, when I first moved in."

The sunflower hulls were back to being possible evidence. The ones she found were dry and intact. The rain they'd had would have turned old ones into mush.

"Back to the security system—any recommendations?" Boyd's question broke into her thoughts.

"How about asking Reese to do it? He's reliable and honest."

"Good call. He seemed like a competent guy," Boyd said. "Do you have his number?"

Kaylee recited the digits while he typed them into his phone. "He does all the work at the shop and at my home. That's why I have his number memorized."

Boyd didn't comment as he made the call. Kaylee was glad. She got enough teasing and innuendo about Reese from Mary and the other Petal Pushers. She concentrated on driving while he made arrangements for Reese to come over that afternoon.

Boyd sighed deeply as he put away his phone. "Even that call took a lot out of me. It's going to be a few more days before I'm back up to speed."

"Don't push yourself," Kaylee warned. "It's important to take time to heal."

Boyd settled back against the seat with a grunt. "I suppose. And just when the story was getting some traction . . ." His voice trailed off as they pulled into the pharmacy parking lot to pick up Boyd's pain medication.

"Why don't you stay here and I'll run in for you," Kaylee said. "Anything you need besides the prescription?"

"I think that's it. Thanks, Kaylee."

"No problem. I'll be back in a jiffy."

With only one pharmacist and a line five customers deep, it took a little longer than a "jiffy." When Kaylee returned to the Escape, she found Boyd had dozed off as he waited. She tried to close her door quietly, but the sound still stirred him from his sleep.

"Sorry," she said as she handed him the paper bag with his prescription in it. "Didn't mean to wake you." She started the car and resumed their drive to the cottage.

"No worries." Boyd straightened up a little, wincing as he did. "Hey, I was thinking. Could you and Reese help me continue searching the property? That money has to be there. And with the news about Butler's skeleton getting out, I don't want to dawdle."

The answer was easy. "Absolutely. I mean, I can't speak for Reese, but I bet he'd love to help. We're both fascinated by the story of Edna and the bank robber. And now Jack Butler's murder." Kaylee took the opportunity to share what she'd gleaned from Edna's papers, starting with the bank account.

Boyd whistled. "She closed her account at the bank right before it was robbed? That is certainly telling."

"That's what I thought. Granted, it might be a coincidence." Kaylee didn't believe that, not when one of the bank robbers had headed for Edna's house. "And get this—I think she was involved with Lester." She relayed the contents of Maisie's letter.

The writer groaned and Kaylee glanced over, concerned. He saw the look and chuckled. "I'm all right. I'm just stunned by this story. It keeps getting better and better." He pointed at her. "I definitely want you on board. I'll credit you as one of my researchers."

After experiencing the cutthroat nature of academia, Kaylee

appreciated Boyd's offer to give her credit. "That's generous of you. Frankly, I'm fascinated. Since Edna's business used to be in my shop, I feel somehow connected to her story."

Boyd beamed. "With any luck, we'll find the missing loot. And I just know this book will be a best seller."

"A friend of mine owns a bookstore here. I'm sure she'd be happy to help you promote it," Kaylee offered.

"Is that Between the Lines? Great shop. I'd love to do some promo work there."

They discussed ideas the rest of the way back to Buttercup Cottage. Kaylee noticed with a lift of her heart that Reese's truck was already parked in the drive.

"He is reliable," Boyd said. "Right on time." Once Kaylee parked, he got out of her vehicle, moving slowly. Reese came hurrying to help, but Boyd waved away his assistance. "I'm all right. A little woozy when I stand up suddenly." He grinned at Reese. "Thanks for getting here so quickly."

Reese cast a worried glance at Kaylee. "I moved things around and hurried over. I figured this was a priority."

"I appreciate it." Boyd plodded carefully to the house, Kaylee and Reese following closely. He foraged in his pocket for his key. "Come on in. I'll put on coffee."

Kaylee hadn't been inside the house, and she looked around curiously. The decor was distinctly old-fashioned, featuring floral wallpaper, chintz-covered furniture, and lace curtains. Had Edna made those? But large, multipaned windows let in the light, and the dark woodwork was in remarkably good condition for a place this old and neglected.

"The people next door kept the place up pretty well," Boyd said as he moved around the vintage, but spotless, kitchen making coffee. "The last person who lived here was Paul's grandmother. After she passed, they decided to sell."

"It's cute," Kaylee said. Then, chiding herself for being distracted by the cottage's charm, she shook her head. "Boyd, you've just been released from the hospital. You should sit down. I'll make the coffee."

"Thank you," he said with a mixture of reluctance and relief, perching on a chrome-trimmed chair.

Meanwhile, Reese went back out to his truck and carted in several boxes. "I picked up the parts for the security system at Get Wired. Now I just need to install it." While Kaylee listened, the two men discussed the various components, cameras, sensors, and alarms.

"That's going to be the most modern thing in here," she said with a laugh, adding milk to the coffee Boyd handed her.

Boyd nodded. "I'm afraid that's true."

"Speaking of which, you'll be able to monitor your alarm system from your computer or your phone," Reese said. "So if you're away from home, you'll know when there is an intruder before you get that call from the sheriff."

Kaylee's phone buzzed. She picked it up with a laugh. "It's Mary, not my alarm company." She stepped into the living room to take the call and explained she was still with Boyd at the cottage.

"I hoped you were out there," Mary said. "Can you pick up a dozen pots of mums at the farm? I just had a customer wipe us out."

"Sure." Kaylee checked the time. "I should be back at the shop before closing. How's Bear doing?"

"He's wonderful." Mary's tone was fond. "He keeps trying to get me to give him treats, the little darling."

"At least make him earn them by doing some tricks," Kaylee said with a chuckle. After she disconnected, she returned to the kitchen, where Boyd and Reese were poring over a map. She filled them in on her planned errand.

"Would it be possible for you to come back after buying the mums?" Boyd asked. "I have another idea where the treasure might be." He pointed to the map. "There are two well houses on this property. The newer one was built during the 1920s when the other spring dried up."

"I'd love to check it out," Kaylee said. "But I do need to get back to the store by five to pick up Bear."

"How about this? I'll get started on the alarm while you run over to the farm," Reese said. "When you get back, we'll go check out the well house. We should have time before it gets dark and before you have to head back. I'll finish up after you leave to get Bear." He turned to Boyd. "Your system will be operational before I leave tonight."

"Sounds like a plan." Kaylee headed for the door, eager to get back and help search for hidden treasure.

A few minutes later, Kaylee pulled to a halt in the farmyard. She noticed that the place had a deserted, lonely air, as if Violet had taken its heart when she left. A couple of other customers were there, poking through the diminished bins of fresh vegetables or looking at the drooping perennials in pots, but there was a hushed gloom, as if they felt the way Kaylee did.

Paul moseyed aimlessly around the barn. He didn't notice Kaylee until she was standing right in front of him.

"I'd like to buy a dozen mums," she said. While she waited for a reply, her gaze fell on the display of seeds and herbs. Had the sunflower seeds she'd found come from this farm? She grabbed a bag to compare. "And this too. And I think The Flower Patch might have a balance due for all the pumpkins we've been buying."

"Okay." Paul finally appeared to tune in. "I'll ring it all up, and you can pick whichever mums you want."

Mary hadn't designated a color, so Kaylee decided on four each of white, gold, and burgundy. While Paul was processing her card, she tried to break his glum silence by asking, "How are you today?"

He slid the receipt and a pen across the counter. "Not so great." He chewed at his lower lip, now edged by a dark three-day beard. "Ever make a huge mistake, one that can't be taken back? And then the worst thing that could possibly happen does, and you know you have no one to blame but yourself? Because that's how I am."

A woman stormed into the main space from a side area, and Kaylee recognized Paul's sister, the manager of the Tortoiseshell Hotel. "Of course he's not good," Charlie said, scowling. "His wife just walked out on him. Not that it's any great loss, in my opinion."

Paul put up a hand. "Charlie, please. Let's not air our private business."

In response, Charlie's frown deepened. "Kaylee was here when she left. You told me that. Not that Violet had any reason to go. Just because you shut down her harebrained—"

Kaylee realized that Paul must have been watching when she came to pick up the pumpkins. How humiliating for him. "Look, it's okay. It's none of my business."

"Nonsense. Why shouldn't you know? Everyone should know what a horrible—"

"Charlie. Enough." Paul's voice was a low growl.

His sister was undeterred by his annoyance. "Quit blaming yourself. You're better off without her."

"I'm sorry, but I've got to get going." Kaylee took her receipt and slipped out of the barn. Attempting to block out their continuing argument, she hurriedly picked out her mums. To distract herself, she mulled over Paul's statement about making a mistake. Was he referring to Violet leaving or something more sinister? Perhaps he *had* attacked Boyd out of jealousy over his wife. The farm's proximity to the cottage meant the farmer could easily have slipped through the woods, hit Boyd, and run home again.

And what harebrained scheme had Violet proposed? That was something else to wonder about.

Kaylee stowed the pots of flowers in the backseat and rear cargo area. The soil was moist enough that they should be fine for a couple of hours. She put the sunflower seeds into her purse, planning to compare them to the sample she'd taken in the woods.

Back at the cottage, Boyd was watching from the porch while Reese mounted a sensor to the front doorframe. They turned to wave as Kaylee drove up and parked. She left the windows open to keep the flowers cool and climbed out.

Reese grinned as she approached. "Ready for our adventure?" He slid his tools back into the holster. "I've got the doors done and the panel up so far. I'll do the windows, motion detectors, and programming when we get back."

"He's fast," Boyd said. He pointed to a rusty shovel and the metal detector resting against the outside wall of the house. "Those are what we're going to use at the well house. Sorry about the wobbly shovel head. It's practically as old as the cottage, which is why I borrowed Kathy's." He patted his pocket. "I've also got a flashlight with me."

Kaylee picked up the shovel, allowing Reese to carry the metal detector since Boyd wasn't up to lifting or digging yet. But he did guide them to the well house, located across a field behind the house. The dilapidated wooden structure was practically buried in a thicket of bramble bushes.

"I take it there's still a little water seeping out of that spring," Reese said with a grimace. "Otherwise those bushes wouldn't be quite so healthy."

"Sorry about that," Boyd said. "I haven't been back here before."

"Let me go get my brush cutter," Reese said. "Otherwise

Kaylee and I will be ripped to ribbons by those thorns." He laid the metal detector in the grass and loped back to his truck.

Kaylee and Boyd waited in silence for a minute, the only sound being late crickets in the grass. "I had a strange encounter with Paul Moore today," she said. She told him what Paul had said and about Violet leaving the farm. "Do you think one of them attacked you?"

Boyd looked taken aback. "I hate to think so. I mean, Violet and I go way back. And Paul's a good egg."

For a man who wrote true crime, Boyd seemed incredibly blind to the foibles of those around him. "Boyd, someone hit you. If it wasn't Kathy, then the Moores are possible suspects." Kaylee ticked off the points on her fingers. "They live nearby, Violet once dated you, and Paul has a jealous nature, according to Kathy."

Boyd flinched. "I hate to think that. But I have had to discourage Violet's, ah, enthusiasm on more than one occasion. She confided in me that she wasn't happy with Paul." He crossed his arms. "I didn't take advantage, though."

"Some people don't take rejection well." Kaylee could picture a spurned Violet flying off the handle. Had his brush-off hit an unhealed wound? "What happened with her the first time around?"

Boyd rubbed his chin, his gaze fixed on the grass at his feet. "It was such a long time ago . . ."

"Not to Violet, apparently." Kaylee waited, leaning on the shovel.

Boyd sighed. "True enough. She's a lovely woman and fun to be with. But we were never serious. I was never going to fall in love. I made it quite clear from the start, and she understood that. Or at least I assumed she did." His lips curved in a brief, sad smile. "After Kathy and I—well, I never wanted to get that deeply involved again. Once burned and all that."

As Kaylee wondered if Violet had the same memory

of events as Boyd, she saw Reese trotting across the field, carrying his gas-powered brush cutter. "Here comes Reese." She gestured at the well house. "You really think we'll find something in there?"

"I sure hope so," Boyd said. "The outbuildings were a bust."

The two of them stood back while Reese went to work with the roaring cutter. Within a few minutes, he'd cleared a path to the door of the well house, the brambles cut close to the ground. Reese switched off the motor and set the tool aside, then wrenched the swollen, warped door to the well house open.

"Want to take a look?" Reese stepped back and gestured to the dark opening. "After you."

Kaylee also stepped back to allow Boyd to enter first. He turned on the flashlight and shone it around the space, which was barely big enough to hold the three of them. In the center of the room, a pipe extended over an empty cistern.

Kaylee smelled water and earth with a hint of mildew. "Not much room to bury anything in here."

"Good," Boyd said. "We'll be able to eliminate it quickly. Of course, if we do, I'm out of ideas." He rubbed his chin, his brow furrowed. "For the moment."

Reese was outside with the metal detector. "Let me make a circuit with this first, and then we can dig." He waited by the doorway until they came back outside. Boyd left the flashlight propped up so it lit most of the interior.

"There will be pipes at the back of the cistern," Boyd said, leaning over the metal detector and adjusting the settings. "The detector will definitely pick those up." He gave the tool a pat, then straightened. "You're all set."

Kaylee and Boyd stood outside while Reese made methodical passes with the metal detector. "I thought of something else to investigate," she said. "I noticed Lester Clayton has the same last name as the bank president at the time, Orville Clayton. I know it's a long shot, but what if they were related?"

Reese appeared in the doorway, shaking his head. "Left side's all done. Nothing." He moved to the other side of the building.

Boyd was staring at Kaylee in admiration. "I didn't even notice that. Granted, I've just started digging. How would you like a library assignment? I'm not quite up to that yet. Want to see if you can find a link between the two men?"

"Sure. I could do that." Kaylee liked doing research. "Any thoughts how to approach it?"

Boyd smiled. "Oh yes. You can search for either man or both. Look at the census records for 1920 and 1930. Check the databases for births, weddings, and deaths. Then check out the obituaries. Those are good sources of family information. Then do an article search in the Seattle newspaper archives. A man as prominent as Orville would most likely be mentioned."

Kaylee was making notes on her phone. "I'll start with this. If I get stuck, can I call you?"

"You bet. Text or call anytime."

Reese gave a whoop. "I think I've found something." His companions crowded into the well house to watch while Reese demonstrated the reaction of the detector.

"That looks very promising," Boyd said. "It's bigger than a coin or random piece of metal."

"Time to dig." Reese carted the metal detector outside, then returned with the shovel.

Kaylee and Boyd waited outside the tight space while Reese went to work on the packed dirt floor of the shack. "The digging isn't quite as difficult as you might expect," he explained during a brief rest. "It's almost like someone else disturbed the soil."

Kaylee's belly flipped over, thinking of their last discovery. "As long as it isn't another body under there."

"Too much metal," Boyd said reassuringly. "Unless he has metal rods or plates in his bones, that is. And that didn't happen often back then."

"Thanks. That's a huge comfort," Kaylee said drily.

Finally, they heard the shovel strike something with a *clank*. Exchanging glances of excitement, they once again crowded into the well house. Reese's smile, gleaming in the near dusk, greeted them. He pointed at the hole, lit by the flashlight beam. "We've hit pay dirt."

Kaylee watched with baited breath as Reese finished clearing soil from around the sides of a rectangular metal box. Using the shovel, he levered it out of its resting place and carried it outside.

The trio regarded the sizable metal box in silence for a moment. Reese crouched down and rubbed at the crust of dirt and grime with his handkerchief, revealing black paint. He then wiped around the keyhole and the edges of the lid, cleaning under the rim.

"We're probably going to have to break into it," Boyd said. "I'm sure the key is long gone."

"Maybe we can cut off the hinges. I wouldn't want to use a torch if there's money inside." Inserting all his fingers into the crack between lid and box, Reese pulled. He gave a yelp as it gave a little. "It's not locked."

13

Kaylee's heart began to pound. How could it be that easy? Had they really found the robbery loot, hidden for more than eighty years?

"That's a new one on me," Boyd said, watching as Reese continued to pry the box open. "Not locking it, that is. Whoever buried it must have been really sure no one else would ever find it."

Reese grunted. "Lester was planning to go to Canada, right? This was probably only a temporary hiding place." He gave another groan of effort and the lid came fully free. He sat back on the grass with a sigh. "Go ahead, Boyd."

Boyd lifted the lid the rest of the way, his face alight with eagerness. Then he frowned. "It's empty."

Kaylee bent close to peek inside. "Not quite." She plucked a slip of paper from a corner and squinted at the printed words. "It's a bill wrapper." Banks used them to bundle paper money.

"Let me see that." Boyd examined it, then let it flutter to the grass. "You're right. The money *was* here." His shoulders slumped. "But now it's gone."

"Think of it as just another step in solving the mystery," Kaylee said. She pulled out her phone. "Put that back in the box and let's take a picture. It will look good in your book."

She ended up taking pictures of Boyd and Reese by the box, the inside of the well house, and Reese with the metal detector.

On the way back to the cottage, Boyd asked, "How can you be so chipper about this setback, Kaylee? I'm impressed."

She shrugged, not exactly sure herself. "I don't know. I've hit dead ends before, and I kept going anyway. Eventually I got there."

"Listen to her," Reese advised the other man. "I've learned it's a good idea."

Kaylee picked up an egg and cracked the shell. The whites needed to be at room temperature, according to the macaron recipe. She hoped that she'd waited long enough. She had set the eggs out that morning before church, and she'd forced herself not to touch them all afternoon. From a kitchen chair, Bear watched, cocking his ears when he heard the distinctive sound of eggshells fracturing.

"Yes, Bear, your owner is actually trying to bake," Kaylee told him with a laugh. She carefully separated the whites from the yolks, saving the latter for scrambled eggs. The remaining ingredients waited on the counter, including almond flour, flavoring, and two kinds of sugar. A piping bag and baking trays lined with parchment paper awaited the fragile batter she was carefully preparing.

Outside the cozy kitchen, the early November night had fallen, and a rising wind howled around the house. Rain was in the forecast.

Kaylee picked up the hand mixer. Before she could lower the beaters into the bowl of egg whites, however, her phone rang from the counter nearby. With a glance at the screen, she saw that her grandmother was calling. Kaylee hesitated, wanting to mix the cookies but hating to let Bea's call go to voice mail. Finally, she picked up. "Hi, Grandma. Can I call you back in a few minutes? I'm making macarons." She gave the word a French flair.

Bea laughed. "I haven't made those in years, since you were in high school. Are they for the bake sale?"

"Yes they are. Well, actually, these are my test batch."

"I'll let you go then so you can focus. Be careful not to overmix when you're incorporating the flour."

Kaylee smiled. "Thanks for the reminder. I'll be careful."

"I'm sure you will, dear. But please do call me back. I heard Kathy Fitz got arrested for attacking Boyd. I've been in shock ever since."

"It is hard to believe." Kaylee's heart sank, the way it did whenever she remembered the event. "And the arrest is partly due to me seeing her drive away from the direction of Boyd's place."

She glanced down at the waiting egg whites. "I'll tell you all about it when I call back in a few." Not wanting to hang up on a somber note, she added, "On another topic, Reese and I dug something up this afternoon at the cottage. I'll give you the details in a bit." She smiled at Bea's indignant squawk as she disconnected.

After beating the eggs into fluffy peaks, she folded in the sifted almond flour and powdered sugar. This is where it could all go wrong, if she mixed the batter too much or too little, but she did her best to follow the recipe's—and Bea's—instructions. Finally, she piped circles of batter onto the baking trays to set.

"I've got half an hour," she said to Bea when she called her back. "Then I need to put the cookies in the oven." She heard rustling sounds in the background as Bea settled into her favorite chair with a cup of tea. She'd witnessed that in person more times than she could count.

"Let's talk about what you and Reese discovered first. I've been dying of curiosity."

"It's more we discovered something missing." Kaylee went over the events of the afternoon and then the conversation moved to the skeleton. "It looks like the two thieves had a fight on Blossom Island, where Jack used to live as a child, and Lester killed him."

"Awful. I never understood why Lester went to Orcas. Why didn't he head for Canada?"

Kaylee thought of the letter from Maisie Fitz. "I think he and Edna might have been involved." She found the letter and read it to Bea, thinking that she really ought to take the paperwork to Boyd. She'd forgotten earlier that day.

"Maisie Fitz," Bea said when Kaylee was finished reading. "She was Kathy Fitz's grandmother."

"I wondered if they were related. So who do you think Maisie was talking about?"

Bea was silent for a minute. "I can see why you think it might have been Lester. But it could have been anyone. Seattle was a big place, even back then."

"So why did he go to Buttercup Cottage?" Kaylee groaned, feeling like she was going in circles. "And if he hid the money there, who took it?"

"I'm sure you'll figure it out," Bea said. "Keep digging."

Kaylee wasn't as certain. How could they find out the truth about something that happened so long ago? It wasn't like any of the witnesses were still alive. "We can't even figure out who hit Boyd on the head."

Bea's sigh was loud enough for Kaylee to hear it. "Tell me about Kathy. Why do they think she did it?"

"A combination of things." Kaylee laid out the sheriff's case. "To be honest, I'm wondering if Violet Moore or her husband had something to do with it." She relayed the odd behavior the couple had been displaying.

"If their fingerprints weren't on the shovel, they must have been wearing gloves. I don't like the sound of that."

Bea was right. That spoke of deliberation. Then why hadn't the assailant made sure Boyd was dead? Giving him only a tap on the head risked far too much.

The timer went off. "I'd better go," Kaylee said. "Time to put the cookies in the oven."

"Keep me posted, okay? I'd hate to see Kathy go to jail. She's a lovely person."

"I will, Grandma. Hopefully we can find the real culprit. Love you." Kaylee hung up and hurried to the stove. She was eager to see how her first batch of macarons would come out.

"Not bad." Jessica took another nibble of the macaron, then smirked and popped the whole thing into her mouth. "Who am I kidding?" she said after she finished chewing. "It's great!" She picked up another. "They even have feet. You said you did this on your first try?"

Kaylee glowed with pleasure. Her macarons did indeed have "feet," the sign of a proper rising in the oven. This gave the cookie its distinctive airy ridges in the middle of each wafer. Between the top and bottom layers, she'd piped fluffy pumpkin spice buttercream.

"I'm glad you approve," Kaylee said. "I hope I can replicate them for the bake sale." Her glance fell on a woman drinking coffee and reading the paper at a table nearby. When the woman raised her head, she recognized Charlie Moore. She gave her a smile and wave, which Charlie returned.

"Good morning, ladies," a woman's voice said behind Kaylee.

Kaylee turned to see Kathy. With her was a tall, thin man. After a minute she recognized one of the bird-watchers—the one called Ned. Today he wore a trench coat over his chinos and long-sleeved polo. At first, she wondered if they'd merely come into the bakery at the same time, but then Ned edged closer to Kathy.

"What's good in here, babe?" he asked, studying the chalk-board menu behind the counter.

Babe? Kaylee choked back an exclamation. Her eyes met Jessica's, who raised both brows with a shrug.

"Oh, Ned, everything is delicious," Kathy said. She spotted the plate of cookies in Kaylee's hands. "Macarons? My favorite!"

"I'm making them for the bake sale." Kaylee nodded toward the poster advertising Anything But Pie. "Go ahead, have one. And let me get out of your way. I'm all done here."

Kathy snagged a cookie, and then she and Ned pressed into the space Kaylee had vacated. Kaylee was on her way to the door when she remembered Maisie Fitz. She waited near the counter for them to order, which took a few minutes as they debated lattes versus cappuccinos. After they had paid, she said, "Kathy, I have a question for you."

The librarian whirled around, putting one hand to her heart. "You startled me. I didn't know you were still here."

"I shouldn't be. Duty calls." Kaylee tipped her head toward the door. "But I wanted to tell you that I found a letter from your grandmother among Edna Taylor's things. Her business used to be in my shop."

Kathy's eyebrows lifted. "As in Buttercup Cottage's Edna Taylor?"

Ned stepped closer, curiosity on his lean features. Kaylee felt a pang of trepidation. Perhaps she should have waited until Kathy was alone. But why would a tourist from out of town care about old island stories anyway?

"Yes, that Edna," Kaylee said. "She and Maisie were friends, I gathered from the letter."

Kathy nodded. "I think I vaguely remember that. Gram died when I was ten, so I didn't know as much about her as I would have liked."

"I'm sorry to hear that." Kaylee couldn't help but think of Bea. She was so fortunate to still have her. Shaking off the grim thought, she said, "I'd better go. But catch up with me later and I'll show you the letter."

After dropping the cookies off at The Flower Patch, Kaylee headed to the sheriff's office. She had an appointment with Deputy Nick Durham. Although Brooks and Garcia had responded to the call at Buttercup Cottage, Nick often provided investigative support to cases that were going to court.

"How are you today, Aida?" Kaylee asked when she entered the station.

"I'm great, thanks. Looking forward to Thanksgiving." Aida adjusted her glasses and popped another wintergreen Tic Tac into her mouth. Kaylee could almost tell the time of day by how far into her daily pack Aida was. "Love those polka-dot pumpkins in your window by the way. I might buy a few if I'm feeling adventurous."

Kaylee laughed. Aida rarely veered from her standard order of dyed carnations. "Better hurry. They're going like hotcakes." Earlier that morning, Mary told her another inn wanted a dozen pumpkin lanterns for their dining room.

"I will." Aida swiveled her chair to face her computer. "Have a seat. Nick should be right out."

Kaylee had barely sat in a chair when the door opened and Nick beckoned. "Good morning, Kaylee," he said with a smile. Nick was the biggest flirt on the island, but thankfully he'd quickly given up on wooing Kaylee, and they had settled into a sibling-like friendship. He rubbed his goatee with two fingers. "What do you have for me today?"

She patted her handbag. "Some possible evidence in the Parsons case."

Nick's brow furrowed, but he didn't say anything until

they were seated at his desk. He regarded her with a concerned expression. "I know you're friends with Kathy Fitz and a witness to boot, so I'm not going to get into detail about the case."

Kaylee had expected that attitude, but her heart took a dive at the implied reprimand anyway. She preferred it when she was working hand in glove with the department, not pushed to the side. "Fair enough, Nick. I wanted to give you these. It's up to you what you do with them." She placed two clear zip-closure plastic bags on the desk.

He threw her a puzzled glance. "Sunflower seeds? I don't get it."

She pointed at the package with a paper label that said *Buttercup Cottage.* "I found these at Boyd's house, near a window and along the path to the farm. Most of them are still out there. The others are from the farm itself, a new package. They are botanically identical." She'd examined them first thing that morning.

"So? A lot of people eat sunflower seeds." Nick's face creased in a brief grin. "Not me, though. They're too much work."

"Boyd says he doesn't eat sunflower seeds. This means someone else was on the property. It could very well be the person who attacked him."

Nick scoffed. "They could have been sitting there for ages."

She shook her head. "Nope. The ones I found are as crisp as the new ones, which means they landed there recently. Finding them on the path to the farm makes me think the person came through the woods." She shivered, remembering the figure she'd seen watching her. "That would explain why I didn't see a vehicle. They probably parked in the nature preserve somewhere."

Nick picked up a pen and tapped on the desk blotter, thinking. Kaylee didn't say anything else, but she crossed her fingers where he couldn't see, hoping he would come around to her way of thinking.

"All right," the deputy said finally. "I'll take these into

evidence. Who knows? Maybe Kathy is a sunflower seed nut." He reached for a form and uncapped the pen.

"Even if so, she'd park in the yard, not creep through the woods." Kaylee couldn't resist pointing that out. "She and Boyd were on good terms."

"Surprising, isn't it?" he muttered. "Seeing as they had an ugly divorce and all."

The Flower Patch was busy that day with customers getting ready for Thanksgiving. They all wanted floral centerpieces, pots of mums for their front steps, or cute pumpkins for their displays. As they cashed out after closing time, Mary declared herself pleased with the numbers.

"Bea always said you had to shake things up once in a while." She closed the register drawer with a smile. "I think we've done that this year."

"Thanks to you." Kaylee was in the front window rearranging the display to hide the bare spots made by demanding buyers. "Even Aida wants to buy some of these." She held up an adorable white pumpkin covered with pink polka dots.

Mary laughed. "That would be a change." She picked up her handbag and the plate of macarons. "Thanks for letting me take these to Herb. He'll enjoy them." Her husband was a retired mail carrier with a fondness for home-baked treats.

"Tell me what he thinks," Kaylee said, stepping out of the window. "I value his expert opinion."

"I sure will." Mary exited through the back room, calling goodbye to Bear on the way. Tags jingling, he escorted her to the door, then trotted back to Kaylee.

Kaylee bent to give him a pat. "Ready to go home?" She certainly was—almost. Unanswered questions about Edna's life had been nagging at her all day. Who had she been planning to marry? Was she in cahoots with the bank robbers or was she an innocent bystander?

Maybe there was an answer in the attic, a clue she'd missed. Making a last-minute decision, she reached for the treat jar and threw one to Bear. "Sorry, boy, it will be a little while before we eat dinner. I'm going up to the attic again."

Bear accompanied her, his presence a comfort. She appreciated the friendly nudges against her ankles and the scrabbling click of his nails on the wood boards as he leaped from step to step. On the third floor, Kaylee flipped on the light and made her way to the corner where Edna's boxes and trunks were stored. This time, she would go through every tin and box, even the ones she'd assumed held only sewing machine parts, buttons, or scissors.

In the first container, she discovered buttons by the score in a veritable kaleidoscope of colors and materials. She set those aside, thinking some might be valuable or of interest to collectors. Another crate held stacked metal boxes. One by one, she opened them, finding sewing machine feet, bobbins, and cords. The one on the very bottom, tucked under a stray piece of cotton calico, held something else entirely.

A revolver.

Kaylee inhaled with a sharp gasp, shocked that Edna Taylor had owned a handgun. Then she studied the engraving a little more closely. In curly script on the handle were the initials *J.B.*

14

She had no evidence, but Kaylee was positive that the gun had belonged to Jack Butler. Why did Edna have it in the first place? And why had she kept it, hidden in her sewing supplies? Another mystery—one of many, it seemed—in the life of the seamstress.

Kaylee regarded the revolver, which gleamed wickedly in the dim light from the overhead bulb. What should she do with it? She could legally own a handgun in this state, and this antique was now hers since she'd bought the building with all its contents. If she called the police, they might take it into custody for the Jack Butler case. For now, she wanted to keep it around. It might be an important clue in Edna and Lester's story.

In the end, she put the gun in the box and replaced the lid, then tucked it into the crate. She'd be sure to tell Boyd about it when she brought over Edna's papers. He'd want to see it, certainly, but she needed to have Reese make sure it wasn't loaded first.

Calling for Bear, she headed for the stairs. It was well past time to call it a day.

Kaylee's cell phone rang while she was unlocking her car behind the store. Fumbling for it, she dropped her handbag and everything spilled out onto the pavement. Bear trotted after an errant lipstick rolling toward the Dumpster.

She wrenched the phone out of her jacket pocket. "Hello?" she said, crouching to pick up her scattered belongings. The lone light on her building didn't penetrate this far, and she was in almost total darkness. Worse, the gusting wind was making shadowy shapes shift and sway in a nearby cluster of trees. Bear ran in that direction, barking. "Hush, boy. Hello?" she said again.

"It's Reese. Sorry to call last minute, but I was wondering if you'd like to grab a bite at The Ideal Meal tonight." The Ideal Meal was renowned for grilled steak and seafood.

Kaylee considered the contents of her refrigerator. Nothing exciting in there. Then again, even if there had been, she would have ignored it in favor of a meal with Reese. "I'd love to. I'm just leaving the shop, so give me an hour to get home and feed Bear." *And change into something nicer than jeans and a long-sleeved T-shirt.*

"I'll swing by and pick you up." He confirmed the time and hung up.

Anticipation warming her on the cold night, Kaylee gathered the rest of her things, unlocked the door, and stowed Bear inside. As she opened the driver door, something shifted again in the dark. Bear barked and leaped toward the car window.

"Who's there?" Kaylee's excitement curdled into fear.

No one answered. A blast of wind rattled bare branches, making their shadows dance. Kaylee didn't call out again. She jumped in the car, locked the doors, and started the engine.

Indignation invigorated her movements as she peeled off toward home. If people wanted to lurk outside buildings at night, let them. She didn't have time to worry about it. With Bear as her early warning system, anyone would be hard-pressed to sneak up on them. "You're a good boy," she told him. "Thanks for having my back." He wagged his tail at her.

At Wildflower Cottage, Kaylee took care of Bear's dinner, then jumped into the shower with a fresh bar of DeeDee's handmade soap. The creamy lather and calming scent helped her wash away all the stresses and strains of the last few days. For the rest of the evening, she was going to focus on her dinner with Reese and forget stalkers, guns, and mysterious assailants.

Among her winter sweaters, she found a dark-red cashmere tunic that brought out her dark hair and green eyes. With black leggings, ballet flats, and dangly earrings, she had an outfit that was casual but attractive.

Steamy warmth and delectable aromas greeted Kaylee when she stepped into The Ideal Meal, Reese behind her. "Holt," he said to the hostess.

"Party of two?" The tall, young blonde checked off the reservation and gathered two menus. "Follow me."

The upscale restaurant—with its burgundy leather booths, wood paneling, and leafy green plants—was filled with laughing, chattering patrons. The hostess settled them in a cozy booth at the far wall. Kaylee slid into one side, with Reese sitting opposite. Paula, according to her name tag, placed the menus on the table with the assurance their server would be there soon.

"What sounds good?" Kaylee asked Reese, opening her menu.

He grinned. "Everything. But I plan on having my favorite: steak, baked potato, and salad."

"Classic choice."

"It never fails me." Reese's eyes twinkled, and Kaylee thought that his navy chamois shirt made them look even bluer than usual.

Their waitress arrived a moment later. The smiling young woman was petite, with brown curly hair and a spray of freckles across her pert noise. "Hi, I'm Jenny. I'll be your server tonight."

Kaylee recognized her. "You work at Death by Chocolate sometimes."

"I sure do." Jenny's eyes widened. "You have that cute little dog, right?"

"Yes, his name is Bear. I'm Kaylee and this is Reese."

Jenny's smile grew even wider. "I know Reese. T-bone, medium rare."

Reese slapped his menu shut. "Got it in one. Do you know what you want, Kaylee?"

Kaylee's gaze dropped back to the menu. "I'll have grilled shrimp with a baked potato and a salad with house dressing. And iced tea to drink."

"Same sides for me and iced tea also," Reese said. "Thanks."

Jenny bustled off, but returned with the drinks and salads a few minutes later.

"So what's new?" Reese asked, picking up his fork. The salad was a mound of leafy greens topped with ripe tomatoes, cucumber, shaved carrots, and croutons.

"Where to begin?" Kaylee thought over everything that had happened since she'd last seen the carpenter. Had it only been two days ago? "I found a revolver in the attic. I think it belonged to Jack Butler."

Reese choked, patted his chest, and swallowed. He reached for his iced tea and took a long drink. "Sorry. Did you say you found Butler's handgun?"

Kaylee looked at him with concern. "Are you okay?" At his nod, she went on. "I think it's his. It's a .38, I think, with the initials J.B. engraved on the handle. It was tucked in with Edna's sewing supplies. I can't imagine who else it could have belonged to."

Reese pointed his fork at her. "Jack was shot with a .38, remember? The deputy told us that."

"I made the connection too. Do you think he was killed with his own gun?" Kaylee grimaced. "This isn't exactly a mealtime topic."

"We'll drop it. But first let me say this—we could find out." He grinned. "Ballistics."

Jenny arrived at the table, a platter in each hand. Her gaze was curious as she set down the food, and Kaylee wondered if she had overheard their conversation.

"Will there be anything else?" the server asked, waiting with clasped hands.

Reese checked for condiments. "We're all set, thanks." After she hurried off, he said, "I think we scared her." His lips curved in a smile. "We aren't your average customers, that's for sure."

Kaylee picked up her knife and fork to cut into a thick, succulent shrimp. "I couldn't agree more. We're both incredibly intelligent and good-looking to boot."

Reese chortled.

They shared a piece of key lime pie for dessert. Reese was in the middle of a story when his phone trilled. "So there we were, on top of the mountain with the fog rolling in—hold on, let me check that." He dropped his fork and grabbed the phone. "That's the alarm for Boyd's house."

She raised an eyebrow.

Reese flagged down Jenny. "I connected my phone to his system in case it went off sometime when he wasn't home. But he's there tonight, as far as I know." Reese dialed Boyd's cell number, but it went straight to an automated voice messaging service, so they hurriedly paid for their meal and hopped into his truck, setting off toward Buttercup Cottage.

"The sheriff's office will also be notified, won't they?" Kaylee asked. Her delicious dinner now sat like a rock in her stomach. What if they arrived too late and Boyd was hurt worse this time, even—she refused to complete the thought.

"They'll be called if the system isn't reset by the owner. But I want to make sure everything is okay." In the dim light of the dash, Reese's expression was strained, his lips set in a grim line. Kaylee realized he shared her fears.

They fell into a tense silence as Reese expertly navigated

the curvy route to Buttercup Cottage, driving fast but always in control. Kaylee watched the quiet landscape flash by, bright house windows providing spots of cheer on this moonless night.

Very few vehicles were on the road, and Kaylee scrutinized each one that passed. Not that she could easily identify them at night, but that didn't stop her from trying.

Reese pulled into Boyd's yard and braked with a crunch of gravel. Before either of them could get out, Boyd opened the front door. "Reese," he called. "It was only a false alarm."

With slower movements, the duo emerged from the truck and made their way to the house. "We wanted to check on you anyway since it went to voice mail when I called," Reese said. "First time out of the gate and all. Wanted to be sure the system did what it was supposed to."

"Sorry I didn't answer. Service is spotty out here," Boyd said. "Come on in." He stood back to let them enter, gesturing toward the cozy living room, which was warmed by a roaring fire. Both Reese and Kaylee headed for the fireplace to warm up. "Would you like a cup of coffee or tea? I have decaf."

"In a minute, maybe," Reese said. "Tell us what happened." He turned his back to the flames, toasting both sides of his hands.

Boyd returned to an armchair, where a book and papers were spread out on the carpet. A notepad and pen sat on the chair's wide arm. He moved them to the adjacent lamp table and sat.

"I was sitting here working on my notes when the alarm went off," the writer said. "I hadn't heard anyone try to get in, so I went to the panel to check the display for faults in incidents."

"That's remarkably coolheaded of you," Kaylee said. "I would have called the sheriff."

"I've had alarm systems before," Boyd said. "They can go off for all kinds of reasons. Anyway, it was the sensor in the laundry room, that little room just off the kitchen. I turned off the alarm and went to check. The glass was still intact. I did a lap outside and didn't see anything or a sign of anyone trying to break in."

"Did the monitoring service call?" Reese asked.

Boyd nodded. "They did, and I gave them the code word—Edna."

Kaylee knew that the code word established that the homeowner was all right. If he or she didn't say it, or said something else, the service would dispatch law enforcement.

"I'm going to take a look around," Reese said. "Just to make sure."

Boyd rose from his seat. "If you insist. I think it was a branch or the wind. I'll put the kettle on."

Kaylee followed Reese to the front door. "I'm coming with you." When his mouth opened in protest, she said, "I insist. If something happens to you, I'll have to go searching for you."

He shook his head, laughing at her bravado. "All right. I'll fetch a couple of flashlights from the truck."

When he handed her one, Kaylee realized his flashlights were large and heavy enough to function as weapons in a pinch. She followed as he made a circuit around the house, checking under the windows for signs of an intruder.

"I don't see any disturbance," he said, peering at the drifted leaves covering the grass near the foundation. He turned to swing the beam farther into the yard.

Kaylee jumped as his light illuminated a figure. Kathy stood cowering among a cluster of overgrown lilacs.

Recovering her senses, Kaylee took a step toward her friend. "Kathy? What are you doing here?" She'd been warned by the police not to come near Boyd, and yet here she was again.

The librarian shielded her eyes from the light. "Can you please move that?" Reese lowered the beam. "Thanks." Kathy came toward them, her sneakers shuffling through the dead leaves. "I got a text from Boyd asking me to come over."

Reese shifted from foot to foot. "He didn't mention it to us. Did you set off his alarm, by chance?"

Kathy glanced toward the cottage. "His alarm went off? It wasn't me. I just got here."

Kaylee gave a huff of exasperation. For a person proclaiming innocence, Kathy certainly behaved dubiously. "Why were you hiding from us?" she asked.

"I didn't know who you were. I just saw the flashlights." Kathy reached into her pocket and pulled out her phone. "Here. I'll show you his text."

When she held out the phone, Kaylee took it and studied the text, Reese looking over her shoulder. *This is Boyd—my alternate number. Come over if you can. I want to talk,* it read.

"He has two phones?" Reese asked, his tone heavy with skepticism.

Kathy lifted her shoulders. "I don't know. Maybe it's a number he uses for work, and he gets better service with it."

"Let's go talk to Boyd," Reese said. "It's too cold to hang around out here."

The trio began walking across the lawn to the front door. Kaylee saw headlights in the trees and then heard the crunch of tires on the drive.

"We've got company," Reese said. As the vehicle came into view, a rack of lights on top was clearly visible. "It's a cruiser."

Kathy turned and bolted for the woods.

15

Reese craned his neck to watch as Kathy disappeared into the dark. "Where's she going?"

"I'm guessing back to her car," Kaylee said. "The deputies would probably arrest her if she hung around." Although Kathy had shown poor judgment in coming to see Boyd, Kaylee wasn't inclined to report the visit to the police. She'd leave any pressing of charges up to Boyd, if he so chose. And if he'd invited her—well, such a decision wasn't likely.

Reese and Kaylee reached the front door by the time the cruiser pulled to a stop. The doors opened and Deputies Brooks and Garcia stepped out.

"There was a report of a disturbance at this address," Officer Brooks said. Then he did a double take. "What are you two doing here?"

Kaylee and Reese exchanged glances. "We came out to check on Boyd," Kaylee said. "His alarm went off."

Now the deputies looked at each other. "Alarm?" Deputy Garcia's brow creased in puzzlement. "The report didn't say anything about an alarm."

Reese made an after-you motion with his arm. "Why don't you come inside and let's see if we can get this straightened out."

Boyd was exiting the kitchen, a cup of tea in each hand when they entered. He almost dropped the mugs when he saw the deputies following Kaylee and Reese. "Where did you come from?" he asked. Wincing as a drop of hot liquid splashed onto his hand, he hastily set the tea down on the coffee table.

"Someone called into the station that there was a problem

out here," Officer Brooks said. "Specifically that there was an intruder."

Kathy. Kaylee flushed hot then cold as she put the pieces together. Had someone lured Boyd's ex-wife out here and then called the sheriff's department? If Reese and Kaylee hadn't been there, Kathy would have probably been inside when the deputies arrived.

"This is all very strange," Boyd said. "I have no idea who made the call or why. Earlier tonight, I experienced a false alarm with my new system. That's why Reese and Kaylee are here. Reese installed it for me the other day."

"No one was trying to break in?" Deputy Brooks asked.

"Not that I saw," Boyd said. He addressed the others. "Neither of you noticed anything, did you?"

Kaylee squirmed. She didn't want to lie to the deputies. "Actually, we did, um, run into someone outside. Kathy Fitz." She put up a hand as Boyd and both deputies began speaking. "Hold on. She got a text from Boyd asking her to come over."

Deputy Brooks' questioning glance at the writer held the unerring menace of a well-aimed arrow. "Did she now?"

Boyd's cheekbones reddened. "I didn't send her a text. I swear it." He located his phone on the table next to his armchair, hidden under a piece of paper. "Here's my phone. You can check all my messages."

"Do you have another phone?" Reese asked. "The text Kathy got said it was from an alternate."

Boyd shook his head and continued to hold out his phone. Neither deputy reached for it.

"If we need to, we can request your records, Mr. Parsons," Deputy Garcia said. "For now, we'll make a report. Sounds like a prank to me. Someone trying to stir the pot."

More than a prank if Kathy had ended up in jail again. But

Kaylee bit her tongue. Perhaps the deputies didn't regard the incident as serious.

"Where is Ms. Fitz now?" Deputy Brooks asked. "She's breached her bail agreement."

So much for that theory. "She decided to leave right about the time you two arrived."

"Interesting." Deputy Brooks made a note. "Is there anything else we can do for you this evening?"

Boyd shook his head, making his long hair swing. "Not unless you can figure out who's pulling these stunts."

"We'll keep our eyes open. In the meantime, keep us informed if anything else happens." Deputy Garcia moved toward the door, then turned. "And make sure you set your alarm."

After the deputies pulled away, Kaylee and Reese sat down to drink the tea and chat with Boyd. "Were you expecting Kathy tonight?" Kaylee asked bluntly.

Boyd rested his head against the back of the chair with a sigh. "That text wasn't from me. I only have one phone. And the last thing I want to do is get Kathy in more hot water."

"So who *would* want to do that?" Reese asked. "Any ideas?"

Boyd kept his brooding gaze on the crackling fire. "No, I'm afraid not."

His voice didn't quite have the ring of truth, but Kaylee decided not to press him. "On another topic, I've been meaning to bring Edna's papers over for days." She laughed. "I keep coming out this way but somehow I always leave the crate sitting in my living room."

A loud bang sounded from the rear of the cottage, making them all jump. Reese rose from his chair, ready to investigate.

"Don't bother," Boyd said. "I have a loose shutter and when the wind comes from a certain direction, it hits the house."

Reese sat back down, casting worried glances toward the kitchen. "I can fix that for you."

Boyd waved him off. "In the daylight. Tell me, Kaylee, have you found anything of interest among Edna's belongings?"

"Tell him what you found tonight," Reese said.

Boyd straightened in his chair. "Yes, fill me in."

Kaylee smiled at the writer's excitement. "I think I found Jack Butler's gun."

An hour later, Reese drove Kaylee home. "Sorry our dinner out was anything but relaxing," he said as they drove back to Turtle Cove.

Kaylee smiled. "And to think I worried that life on an island would be dull."

"Not with you around," he said under his breath. When she threw him a sharp glance, he grinned. "Not taking it back."

She decided to accept his remark as a compliment. Changing the subject, she asked, "Are you going to California for Thanksgiving?" Reese had grown up in the Los Angeles area and still had a widowed mother and a sister living there.

"Afraid not. I'm too busy right now. I'll go for a week around Christmas. How about you?"

Kaylee told him that she was in the same boat, with most of her family in Florida and Bea in Arizona. "I'm grateful we have the community dinner as an option. Otherwise I'd be pretty pitiful." She pictured herself and Bear alone, dining on frozen turkey potpies.

He laughed. "I'm sure someone would have taken you in."

"That did sound pretty sad, didn't it?" She chuckled. "So, what are you doing?"

"Community dinner. I'm making a big pan of my signature dish—oyster dressing."

"That sounds interesting," she said, meaning the opposite. Despite her uncertainty about his offering, she was still glad Reese would be attending the event.

"Oh, it's good." He drew out the last word. "Wish I could eat it all year round."

"Why don't you? Can't you cook it anytime you want?"

"Nope. Thanksgiving only. That keeps it special."

She could relate to that. Her family had special dishes they enjoyed only on holidays. Her mother made the best pumpkin pie, for instance, and her brother's green bean casserole was amazing.

"Here we are," Reese said, jostling Kaylee from thoughts of her family as he swung the truck into Wildflower Cottage's driveway.

Kaylee felt both relief at getting home and disappointment that the evening was over. "Want to come in for a minute? I've got cocoa."

He pulled the truck up beside her Escape and turned off the engine. "You had me at cocoa."

She opened the truck door and felt a blast of cold air. "Let's hurry. The temps must be dropping like a rock."

Laughing at the cold wind that nipped at their faces, they hurried onto the porch. Kaylee unlocked the door and stood back to let her guest enter first. "Bear is going to be so excited to see you."

Reese stood in the front hallway, glancing around. "Um, Kaylee? It's freezing in here."

Kaylee shut the front door and hurried to his side. She definitely felt frigid currents of air from somewhere. And where was her dog? "Bear! Where are you, boy?" She trotted through the house.

The back door stood wide open. Instinctively she rushed to close it.

"Don't touch the knob," Reese said. He stepped past her and pushed it shut by the wood.

Kaylee froze. "You think someone broke in?" Then her shock was swamped by fear for her beloved pet. "Bear?" she called again, running out of the kitchen. She was rewarded by a faint sound of barking.

She searched through the house, flinging open every door. The barking grew louder when she reached the guest bedroom, then the en-suite bathroom. "I'm here, buddy, I'm here," she crooned. She turned the knob and the little dog flew out, like a missile launched from a gun. Kaylee sank to the carpet, allowing Bear to jump all over her and lick any exposed skin he could find. "Cut it out," she said with a laugh. "Let me check you over."

Reese appeared in the doorway. "Kaylee, I called the sheriff. From the look of the door, someone jimmied the lock." His eyes lit with relief. "I'm glad to see Bear is okay."

A wet tongue lapped Kaylee's cheek. "He appears to be. If he'd hold still, I could be certain." She struggled to her feet, carrying the dog with her. "Let's give him something to eat and drink."

They were on their way to the kitchen when Kaylee realized something. The crate of Edna's papers was gone.

"Who would want Edna's old papers?" Kaylee asked Mary for the third time. She was helping Mary arrange bouquets at the shop the next morning. She bit her lip. "I'm sorry. I guess I'm still not over the shock."

Mary fetched a bucket of fresh roses from the cooler. "That's understandable. Having someone break in is so . . . violating. Did the deputies find any clues as to who did it?"

Kaylee picked up a white rose and trimmed off the bottom leaves. "No, unfortunately. Besides Boyd, I have no idea who would care about those papers. There's nothing in there related to the bank robbery. I checked."

"Maybe there's another reason." Mary sorted through stems of baby's breath to find ones she wanted to use. "Something else to do with Edna's life."

Mary's words struck a chord. "I didn't think of that. When I go to the library later, I'll do some more digging into Edna as well as the bank robbers."

"What's your assignment there again?"

Kaylee clipped leaves off a soft-peach rose. "Boyd asked me to look for a connection between Orville Clayton, the bank president, and Lester Clayton, the bank robber. It was my idea, actually. I thought the names were an odd coincidence."

"You could be right." Mary worked in silence for a minute, then said, "By the way, Herb loved the macarons. He told me to buy a half dozen more at the bake sale tomorrow."

A thrill of alarm ran through Kaylee. She'd totally forgotten about the event the next day. She'd have to devote the entire evening to baking. She sighed. Why had she agreed to participate? *Oh, that's right—it's for a good cause.* "I'll set some aside for him," she told Mary. "I hope I can duplicate my success."

"I'm sure you can. Although they may be a little more difficult tonight." Mary gestured at the rain dripping from the eaves. "Talk about high humidity."

Kaylee remembered Bea saying something about humidity and macarons. She'd have to make a fire to dry out the house, which could get damp during rainstorms.

"I'll come help you," Mary said. "Herb has a youth association meeting tonight so I'm free."

Kaylee felt a rush of relief. "I'd love that, Mary. After dinner?"

"Sounds good. I'll bring over some cranberry apple pie for dessert."

Bear woofed at this and both women laughed. "I think he knows the word 'pie,'" Kaylee said.

After making several deliveries, Kaylee swung by the library. As she walked inside, she felt a pang, realizing Kathy wouldn't be there to greet her. Squashing her disappointment and sadness, she said hello to Tina Littlewood, the assistant librarian. Today the petite, red-haired librarian was sporting tiny pumpkins on each fingernail.

"What do you think?" Tina asked. "These were inspired by your window display."

Kaylee smiled. "That's really neat. Thanks." She set some novels and the cookbook she was returning on the counter. "How's everything going?"

Tina glanced around, checking the location of other patrons. She lowered her voice. "I'm heartsick about Kathy. I keep praying every day that this mess gets cleared up and she comes back." Her green eyes were troubled.

"Me too," Kaylee said. "Keep the faith."

"Thanks, Kaylee. I appreciate your support." Tina began to check in Kaylee's books. "Is there anything I can help you with today?"

"I have some research to do, and I hoped you could help me."

"Sure thing." Tina set the returned books on a cart for shelving. "What are you looking for?"

"Several things. The U.S. census records for 1920 and 1930, the Seattle newspaper archives for those decades, and birth, death, and marriage records for the state of Washington."

Tina tipped her head and regarded her with a frown. "That's odd. I had someone else in here the other day wanting to see those very things."

Kaylee's heart thumped. "Who was it?" It couldn't be a coincidence. Either the discovery of Jack Butler's body had spurred another researcher or someone else was on the trail of the missing bank loot. And they were a step ahead of her.

The librarian shook her head. "I'm sorry, I can't tell you that. Library patron confidentiality rules." She pursed her lips, which were painted a chic mauve that flattered her skin tone. "I shouldn't have said that much."

"Don't worry. I've forgotten already." Kaylee swallowed her disappointment. Kathy might have shared the information, but she wasn't there. And it was partially Kaylee's fault.

"Right this way." Tina led her to the computer stations, where she logged into one of the machines. After Kaylee sat down, Tina explained how to access the various documents Kaylee was seeking. "Thanks to our subscriptions, you can get all this for free. It's really wonderful."

Kaylee had to agree. She pulled out a pad and pen, and set to work. First, she searched the census records for Orville and Lester Clayton. In 1920, Lester had been ten years old, living with his mother, Eunice, father, Orin, and a younger brother, Leonard, in Seattle's famed Admiral District. Now she had his family members. She jotted their names and ages on the pad. The occupation listed for Orin was *Banker*.

In 1930, the family consisted of Eunice, Lester, and Leonard, and now they lived in a more modest neighborhood down by the docks. Had Orin died?

She searched for Orin's name in the death files. He had died in 1925. Out of curiosity, she opened the newspaper archives and entered his name.

The story was startling. Mr. Orin Clayton had committed suicide due to business reversals. Lester's uncle, Orville Clayton, had taken over duties as president at the bank. At that time, banks were often closely held affairs and such a succession plan wasn't uncommon.

Had Lester been seeking revenge for his father's death and the family's financial decline? Kaylee thought the evidence strongly pointed in that direction.

She sent the article to the printer for Boyd, along with screenshots of the census information and Orin's death record. She glanced at the clock on the wall, then sent Mary a text. *Do you mind if I stay at the library another half hour?*

That's fine, came the reply. *Bear and I are holding down the fort.*

Kaylee opened the death database again. She couldn't find Edna Taylor's death anywhere in the state of Washington. Had she gotten remarried? She looked through the marriage records and found one in 1930, between Edna Moore and Rufus Taylor. He had died in 1934.

She was stumped. Then realization trickled in. *Moore.* The Moore family owned the farm, and Buttercup Cottage had once been part of the property. As a family member, it made sense that Edna lived in the cottage. Maybe she'd even grown up there.

"How's it going?" Tina appeared at Kaylee's elbow. "Need any more help?"

Kaylee pushed back from the table. "I've gone as far as I can for now. I'm missing some information."

"Like what?" Tina asked. "Maybe I can help."

"I can't find a certain death record. Since it's a woman, I thought maybe she'd gotten remarried. But I can't find a record of another marriage either."

Tina pressed her lips together. "A local woman? Maybe it's in the paper—but you don't have her name. Shoot."

Something Tina said sparked an idea. Kaylee pulled her chair back up to the computer. "Thanks. I'm going to try something."

Tina chuckled. "I'm glad that helped."

After Tina wandered away, Kaylee searched for *Edna, Turtle Cove, seamstress*. Within a couple of minutes, she found the right article.

What it contained made her eyes widen. "Bull's-eye."

16

That evening, Kaylee shared her discovery with Mary over dessert. "I found an article about Edna's death. And guess what I found out? You'll never believe it. I couldn't believe it myself."

Mary paused, a forkful of pie halfway to her mouth. "Go on. You're killing me here."

"She married Lester Clayton after all. And she left a baby behind." That last bit of information had made Kaylee's heart twist in sympathy. What had happened to the child?

"Oh, that poor thing." Mary set the fork down. "Her bank robber husband was killed in a shootout *and* she had a small child?"

"I'm not sure if the baby was born before the shootout," Kaylee said. "But you're right—it's a tragedy." She brought out her phone and found the pictures of Edna and Lester online. She showed them to Mary. "Here they are. The ill-fated couple."

Mary studied their young faces. "They're both so attractive. It's hard to believe Lester was a bank robber."

"I told you my theory about that. I still think he robbed the bank to avenge his father's ruin and suicide." Kaylee took a bite of pie, which was the perfect combination of sweet and tart. "I wonder if Orville forced Orin out and that's why he killed himself."

"Could be," Mary said. "But no matter the reason, I'm sure Lester was bitter about it, especially given the kind of life it led to for him, his mother, and his brother." She got up from the table and looked at the pans of macarons waiting to go into the oven. "Think these are ready?"

Kaylee had given them extra time to dry. Now she tested

one with a gentle finger. "I think so." She opened the oven door and slid in a pan. "Keep your fingers crossed."

As she gently shut the oven door, her phone rang, an unfamiliar number showing up on the display. "Hello?" she said tentatively.

"Hi, this is Tina Littlewood, from the library. Sorry to bother you so late. I hope you don't mind, but I got your number from your file."

"How can I help you, Tina?" Kaylee held up a finger to let Mary know she wouldn't be long.

"This may sound like a strange question." The assistant librarian paused.

"I enjoy those," Kaylee said encouragingly.

There was a nervous giggle, and then Tina blurted, "Have you talked to Kathy lately? Or seen her?"

Kaylee was startled by the question. "I saw her last night." She didn't say where. "Is there something wrong?"

"That's just it. I don't know," Tina said, her voice teeming with anxiety. "She was supposed to come to my house for dinner. The trustees probably wouldn't like it, but she's my friend. And that's not going to change ever—"

"She didn't show up?" Kaylee interrupted. Uneasiness stirred in her. "Did you try calling her?" She puffed out a gust of air, annoyed at her inane question. "Of course you did."

"Yes, I've called her a bunch of times, sent texts, even went by her house. She's not there. Her car is gone too."

Mary caught Kaylee's eye and mouthed, "What is it?"

"Kathy's missing," Kaylee mouthed back.

Mary gasped and put a hand to her cheek.

Kaylee took a deep breath, trying to steady her racing mind. Maybe there was a perfectly good explanation. "Tina, do you think she went somewhere to get away from all of this unpleasantness and forgot to tell you? You can't get good cell service everywhere in the islands."

"True, but standing me up isn't like Kathy," Tina said. "She's the most trustworthy person I know."

Kaylee thought for a long moment. "Do you think she ran away?" Perhaps the scene at Boyd's last night—with the deputies showing up and Kathy realizing someone had tricked her—had sent her over the edge. She pictured Kathy fleeing on the ferry.

Tina groaned. "I sure hope not. Her bail conditions included staying on Orcas. Besides, Kathy just isn't the type to do something illegal like that. No matter what the cops think she did."

"My immediate reaction is to tell you to call the sheriff, but that won't help, will it? If she did run away, they'll put out a bulletin for her. Then she'll be in even bigger trouble."

"I know." Tina sighed. "I guess I'll wait another day and see if she turns up. If you see her or hear from her, let me know, okay?"

"I will, Tina. I promise." Kaylee hung up and said to Mary, "Tina can't find Kathy anywhere, and she's not answering her phone."

Mary's eyes widened and she gripped the tabletop with both hands. "You don't think she . . ." Her voice trailed off.

"Ran away from the police? I sure hope not." That kind of behavior was nothing like the kind, levelheaded Kathy that Kaylee knew. "If she doesn't show up in a day or two, I will call the sheriff. I'm worried, Mary."

Jessica clapped her hands. "Those look amazing, Kaylee." The bakery owner watched as Kaylee arranged her macarons on three-tier dishes set on a table in front of The Flower Patch.

Kaylee had found the dessert stands among her grandmother's dishes, and the white china provided the perfect complement to the delicate orange cookies.

"Thanks," Kaylee said. She handed an extra one to Jessica. "I think they taste okay too."

Jessica munched, her expressive features radiating her enjoyment and approval. "I'd better watch my back," she joked. "There's a new baker in town."

Kaylee laughed. She pointed at the platters holding Mary's contributions. "Don't forget to try those scones and whoopie pies. They are scrumptious."

The baker dug in her apron pocket and placed some money on the table. "I'll take several of each. All for a good cause, right?"

DeeDee came trotting across the street. "Are those your macarons, Kaylee? They're gorgeous. I want half a dozen."

"At this rate, we won't need customers," Kaylee said. "I plan to buy some goodies from both of you too."

The trio stood chatting and sampling baked goods until some actual customers came strolling down the street. "Oops, I'd better get back," Jessica said. "Jenny is working by herself." She tightened her apron and hurried down the sidewalk.

DeeDee waved at a couple standing in front of her table. "Me too. See you later." Halfway across the street she stopped dead and called, "Did you hear the news? Kathy Fitz ran away."

"Where did you hear that?" Kaylee asked. She prayed Kathy hadn't been labeled a fugitive. Not a good move when pleading innocent.

DeeDee shrugged. "I suppose you could call it a rumor. But no one has seen her." She darted to her table and greeted the bake sale customers with a big smile.

Kaylee slumped into the folding chair behind her table.

Her anxiety about Kathy rose from a low-grade hum to a roar. Concern for Kathy's whereabouts had obviously spread beyond Tina. She must have left Orcas.

Mary popped out of the store. "Are you okay out here alone for a while? I figure we can take shifts."

"That sounds fine." Kaylee zipped her fleece jacket up a little higher against the chill. "At least it's not raining." In fact, she discovered that if she moved the chair a little to the right, some of the late-autumn sun touched her face. At this time of year, she was grateful for every ray of sunshine.

Enough customers came by that Kaylee didn't have time to brood about the missing librarian. The Flower Patch table was cleaned out in record time, down to one lone whoopie pie at the end of her shift. Kaylee eyed the treat. If she ate it, then Mary wouldn't have to come out here at all.

A man wearing a ball cap and windbreaker came up to the table. He reached for his wallet. "I'd like to buy that whoopie pie." He grinned, an expression that lit up his angular face. He had very pale gray eyes.

Jessica came bouncing along the sidewalk. "How are you—" She broke off when she saw Kaylee was waiting on a customer.

Kaylee put the treat into a bag and accepted the man's money. "Have a great day."

He saluted in return and made his way down the street.

"I can't believe it," Kaylee said. "We're all sold out and it isn't even noon."

Jessica grabbed Kaylee's arm, her gaze still on the man in the windbreaker. "Do you know who that was?"

"A whoopie pie lover?" Kaylee picked up the cashbox. "Good thing he got here when he did."

"Kaylee. Listen." Jessica's voice was tense. "That was Eldon Landis."

"Should I know who that is?" Kaylee studied her friend's face, puzzled by her intensity.

"He's the man Boyd cleared in that big jewelry heist, the one he wrote about in his best-selling book. What is Eldon doing on Orcas?"

Kaylee didn't have much time to ponder Jessica's question. After moving the bake sale setup inside, she and Mary were swamped with orders and walk-ins. It was as if everyone had realized that Thanksgiving was just over a week away.

Five minutes before closing time, the door opened and Eldon Landis walked in. "Good afternoon," Mary said, greeting him with a smile. "Welcome to The Flower Patch."

He stood just inside the doorway, glancing at the feminine and floral decor in obvious discomfort. "Nice place you got here. But actually, I need to talk to Kaylee Bleu."

"That's me," Kaylee said. "What can I do for you?" She studied the man curiously, remembering that, despite his innocence in the heist, he was a convicted felon. His demeanor and movements were calm, but behind them was an air of quiet menace. His pale eyes reminded Kaylee of a snake coiled to strike.

Eldon took a few steps toward the counter. "I'm looking for Boyd Parsons. Someone told me you could help me."

Kaylee tilted her head. "Who told you that?"

"The lady down at the library said you were doing research for him. So I figured you'd know where he lives."

Since Tina never would have given out that information, it must have been one of the volunteers. Kaylee had no idea why this man wanted to see Boyd, so she erred on the side of caution. "Tell you what. Give me your name and a contact number, and I'll pass it along." She shrugged. "That's all I can do."

He scoffed. "He'll want to see me, all right. I'm Eldon Landis. A very good friend of his."

Mary sent Kaylee a wide-eyed look. In response, Kaylee gave her a tiny nod that said yes, he was *that* Eldon Landis.

"I'm sure that's true," she replied to Eldon out loud, hoping she sounded firm. "But I can't just hand out a friend's home address to someone I don't know. I'm sure you understand. Now, what's your number?"

Eldon pulled out a phone and read off the digits while Kaylee scrawled them on a scrap of paper. "I'm staying at the Northern Lights Inn, Room 302."

"I'll give him a call in a few," Kaylee said.

"Good enough." Eldon gave them a brisk nod goodbye and shuffled toward the door.

As soon as he walked down the street, Kaylee pulled out her phone and called Boyd.

"Good afternoon, Kaylee. Any luck on the research front?" Boyd chuckled. "You've been turning up the best information. I may have to make you a coauthor."

"I did learn something new about Edna, and I'll get to that in a minute." Kaylee felt Eldon's appearance overshadowed any historical clues. "Eldon Landis is trying to find you. He's here on the island."

Boyd was silent for a long moment. "Old Eldon is here, is he? I wonder what's up."

"Me too," Kaylee said. "Wasn't he the guy you got released from prison?"

"That's him. I suppose I should talk to him, see what he wants." Boyd laughed again. "Hope it's not money. I won't have much of that kicking around until I write my new book."

Kaylee gave him Eldon's phone number and lodging information. Then she filled him in on what she'd learned about Edna's marriage and the Clayton family. "I have several articles to show you."

"Can you bring them by later? Perhaps you'd like to listen in while I talk to Eldon."

Kaylee's pulse gave a swoop before kicking into high gear. "Is it safe?" she managed to squeak out.

"Eldon won't hurt you. Or me. He's too grateful that I got him a reprieve from life in prison."

"I hope you're right. See you later." Kaylee disconnected, and before she could talk herself out of it, dialed Reese.

Later that evening, Kaylee's stomach was in a knot as Reese drove them to Boyd's cottage. "I hope Boyd is right," she said for the third time. "I pray Eldon isn't planning to hurt him."

"He'll have to deal with me first," Reese said, his tone grim. He glanced at her and offered a warm smile. "We'll be okay."

They reached Buttercup Cottage before Eldon, which Reese had planned. Boyd answered the door, appearing relaxed and cheerful. "Come in, come in. Would you like something warm to drink?"

"I'll take tea," Kaylee said, and Reese agreed. Boyd excused himself to the kitchen while they made themselves at home.

As on the other night, a fire was roaring, releasing welcome warmth into the snug room. Boyd had pulled long drapes against the night, making the room even cozier. Kaylee thought they looked familiar. She stepped over to the window and felt the green fabric between her fingers. Yes, it was fine, thick velvet, like the ones in her attic.

Boyd came into the room with a tray. "Nice curtains, aren't they?" he said. "They're as old as the hills, but the fabric is still in good condition. I found them tucked away in a closet."

"I found similar ones in my attic at the shop. My guess is they were all made by Edna," Kaylee said. "You can have mine for spares, if you want." She settled in a chair and accepted the cup of tea Boyd handed her.

"I'd appreciate that," Boyd said. He handed Reese a cup too, then moved milk and sugar within reach. "A few of these are a little faded by the sun."

Someone knocked on the front door. Kaylee started, slopping tea over the edge of the mug. She dabbed at her spotted jeans with a napkin, taking deep breaths to calm her racing nerves.

Boyd rose to his feet, ready to answer, but Reese intercepted him. "I'll go."

The writer sank back into his chair, a bemused expression on his face. "You folks really watch out for your friends, don't you?"

"Reese is wonderful that way," Kaylee said while the man in question strode to the front door. From where she sat, she could hear the door open and the low murmur of men's voices.

A few seconds later, Reese and Eldon entered the living room. Eldon had removed his cap, revealing a large, balding head. "Boyd. Good to see you."

Boyd rose from his chair in a lithe move and crossed the room in a couple of steps. He clasped Eldon's hand and patted him on the back with the other. "Eldon. Welcome to Orcas Island." He put both hands on Eldon's shoulders and studied the visitor's face. "How have you been, man?"

A shy smile flitted across Eldon's thin lips. "I'm fine, thanks." He glanced around. "Nice digs."

"It's not too bad." Boyd ushered his guest to a chair. "Want a cup of tea? Or I can put on a pot of coffee if you'd like."

"No, tea is fine." Eldon turned his cap in his thick fingers and cleared his throat awkwardly. He watched as Boyd poured him a cup from the teapot.

"What is it, Eldon?" Boyd asked. "I can tell something is on your mind."

The other man's gray eyes were somber. "You might say that. I'm here to tell you that your life is in danger."

17

A gasp escaped Kaylee's mouth. Eldon's statement raised the possibility that Boyd had been attacked by an unknown assailant, not Kathy. "Do you think that's who hit you?" she blurted.

"Hit you?" Eldon frowned. "Did Brown's henchman get here first?"

Boyd pointed to his head, which no longer sported a bandage. "Someone beaned me on the head the other day. I didn't see who it was, but my ex-wife was arrested."

Eldon smirked. "Gotta watch out for those ex-wives. They can be dangerous."

"Who is Brown?" Reese put in before Kaylee could protest in Kathy's favor. "The criminal you put in jail, Boyd?"

The writer rose from his chair and went to the fireplace. He bent to put another log on the fire. "That's right. Curtis Brown took Eldon's place behind bars."

"That's why I owe you a big one," Eldon said. "The cops, my attorney, the press—they all decided I was guilty the minute I was arrested." He jiggled a knee, sipping at his tea in short bursts.

In contrast, Boyd appeared oddly calm. "Curtis paid a witness to identify Eldon. Now that witness has disappeared." He picked up the iron poker and pushed the logs into place. Sparks flew up the chimney.

"Convenient," Reese said drily.

"He's not a very nice guy." Eldon squinted at Boyd. "You don't seem all that concerned."

Boyd returned to his seat. "I'm saving my nervous breakdown for when he shows up. Any idea who Curtis is sending?"

Eldon fished in his pocket and pulled out his phone. "Actually, yes. One of my contacts sent me this." He held the phone screen outward. "Here they are. Ned and Flint, they're called."

"The bird-watchers?" Kaylee was so stunned, she could barely speak.

The three men stared at her.

"That's what I thought they were, since they were carrying binoculars," she explained. "Boyd, they were at the farm the first day I met you. Since then, I've seen them all over the island."

"Interesting." Eldon stroked his chin as he considered this information. "They must be stalking you, Boyd. I figured they would come in, do the job, and bail."

His matter-of-fact manner sent a wave of cold fear over Kaylee. She had been in close proximity to the two men several times, never guessing their criminal background or evil intent.

Reese's face had gone white. "You've talked to these men, Kaylee?"

She waved a hand. "I couldn't avoid it. They came to the shop and I've seen them at the hospital and at Death by Chocolate." She remembered something else shocking. "Kathy was at the bakery with Ned."

"You mean on a date?" Boyd barked the words and in his horrified expression, Kaylee saw that he still cared deeply for Kathy.

"Sort of. They were drinking coffee together. He called her 'babe.'" The idea that floated into her mind was so terrible she could barely get it out. "What if Kathy is with Ned? And that's why she's missing?"

Boyd jumped up from his chair. "Missing? What are you talking about?"

Kaylee ran both hands through her hair. So much had been happening she couldn't keep straight who knew what. "Her assistant librarian called me last night and told me she hasn't been able to get ahold of Kathy. She—we—thought maybe she ran away. Went off island."

The writer began to pace, his fists clenched at his side. "Did you call the sheriff?"

Kaylee hunched over in guilt, arms holding her middle. "No. I was afraid to get her in more trouble. What if we're wrong and she's just avoiding people right now?"

Boyd whipped out his phone. "She'll speak to me, no matter what kind of snit she's in." He punched the contact then put the phone to his ear. After a minute, his handsome features twisted in disgust. "The mailbox is full."

Eldon was lounging back in his chair, arms crossed. He studied Boyd with bemusement. "I think you still care for this broad. Your *ex*-wife, you say? Could have fooled me."

"Of course I care for her." Boyd's mouth twitched in anger. "We're very good friends. I can't bear the thought that I might have brought trouble to her doorstep." He shoved the phone back into his pocket and began pacing again.

"Hold on," Reese said. "We have no proof that Kathy is in any kind of danger. Or that she ran away to evade justice." He nodded at Kaylee. "Maybe she's holed up somewhere, getting her head together."

Kaylee considered the woman she'd known since moving to the island. Kathy had always seemed sensible. She'd been the island librarian for close to two decades, that in itself a testament to her stability.

"You're right, Reese," she said, already calmer after listening to him. "But let's tell the sheriff she seems to be missing. Maybe they can use their resources and locate her."

"I can handle that." Boyd pulled out his phone again. Then he hesitated. "I'm not supposed to have contact with Kathy."

"Me neither, really," Kaylee said. "Since I'm a witness." She thought for a second. "Let me call Tina. She can file the report."

"Perhaps the fact that she's been fraternizing with a known criminal will light a fire under the sheriff," Boyd said. His expression was bleak. "I hope she's all right."

Soon after, Reese and Kaylee left for home. Eldon had insisted on staying with Boyd "for the duration," a decision Kaylee heartily agreed with. He'd moved his rental sedan to the barn so as not to tip off any unwanted visitors.

They were silent for the first few miles, both lost in their thoughts. "I'm having trouble absorbing all we've heard tonight," Reese finally said. "Criminals sent on a hit? I feel like I'm in a crime show."

"Me too." Kaylee stared out into the night, wondering where Ned and Flint were staying. If only they had mentioned it to her. They certainly put on a good act of pretending to be harmless tourists. Now she was reviewing everything in light of her new knowledge.

"Do you think they're the ones who almost ran us over?" she asked. "Coming back from the island?" Maybe they were also responsible for rear-ending her car, breaking into her home, and lurking behind her store. But why would they want Edna's papers? That part didn't make sense.

"Maybe," Reese said. "I thought at the time that it was deliberate, to harass or scare us. We certainly gave them enough warning."

Kaylee thought about that foggy evening. The other boat had seemed menacing, almost sinister, as it approached so relentlessly. A shiver ran through her body.

"Are you okay?" Reese asked, worry in his voice.

She attempted a laugh. "I'm fine. It's a cold night, that's all."

He reached out and turned up the heat. "I'm going inside your house first and checking it out. Don't try to argue."

Kaylee leaned against the window, his concern as warm and welcome as the air now blasting from the vents. With any luck,

Ned and Flint would soon be arrested, Kathy found and cleared, and the island returned to peace and safety.

"Those two goofy tourists are hit men?" Mary adjusted her glasses as if trying to get a better look at the situation. "I must say, they used an effective disguise."

"I know." Kaylee opened the cooler and reached for a bucket of orange, yellow, and red zinnias, Bear studying her every move. "You expect hit men to seem scary." A fleeting thought made her hand slip off the metal container. *Eldon fits the bill in that department better than Ned or Flint.* She shoved the idea aside and took a firmer hold on the bucket. What was she thinking? Eldon was Boyd's friend.

"Thanks," Mary said when Kaylee set the zinnias beside the worktable. She consulted her list. "Can you please pull out the sunflowers, daisies, and lilies too? We have several Thanksgiving arrangements to make."

While Kaylee was retrieving the flowers, Mary answered a phone call. "Good morning, The Flower Patch. How may I help you?" She listened for a couple of minutes, jotting down an order. When Kaylee brought over the buckets, she was staring at the form, appearing puzzled.

"What is it, Mary? Can we fill the order?"

Mary shook her head impatiently. "It's not that. We have everything in stock." She sighed. "That was the new manager for the Tortoiseshell Hotel. Charlie quit."

Kaylee was taken aback. "Really? I saw her at her brother's farm during business hours, but I didn't realize she wasn't still working at the inn."

"Charlie has always been close to her brother. I'm not surprised she's providing him moral support. But leaving her job? That is odd." Mary began to sort through the flowers, selecting the ones she wanted to use.

The bells on the door jingled and Tina walked in. "Hi, ladies," she said. "I need to order flowers and talk to Kaylee, so here I am, killing two birds with one stone."

"Did you call the sheriff last night?" Kaylee asked, grabbing the order pad. Tina hadn't answered her call so she'd sent a text.

Tina nodded, making her dangling turkey earrings sway. "I sure did. When you called, I was checking Kathy's house again. She wasn't home, and her mail is piling up."

"That's not a good sign."

"That's what I thought." Tina smoothed her hair in a nervous gesture, displaying nails painted with tiny autumn leaves. Her green eyes filled with tears. "I'm so worried." Bear, sensing distress, trotted over and leaned against Tina's ankles in a gesture of comfort.

Kaylee suppressed her own worry and tried to reassure the other woman. "No news is good news, right? She must be okay or we'd have heard."

"What did the sheriff say?" Mary snipped flower stems, wielding the clippers decisively.

"They're issuing a watch bulletin for her," Tina said. "Her car is gone too, so they're extending it to the entire state." She lifted her arms in a helpless gesture. "All we can do is pray." She noticed Bear at her feet and bent to pat him.

"And we will," Mary said. "Kaylee, why don't we give her the special?" The special was The Flower Patch's code for giving customers more flowers than they paid for, often used in times of tragedy or difficulty. Over the years, the special treatment had resulted in deep loyalty and many referrals.

"Agreed." Kaylee picked up a pen with a smile. "What can we get you?"

Tina ordered a couple of arrangements and bought three pumpkin lanterns too, claiming they were "too cute." On the way out the door, she promised to display them at the library for patrons to admire.

"If this keeps up, we'll need yet another load of pumpkins," Mary said.

"You gotta make hay while the sun shines," Kaylee said, filing Tina's credit card slip. "And it's shining on those pumpkins." Bear's nails clicked on the wood behind her as he shadowed her movements. "Hang on, Bear. It's almost treat time."

Mary carried a completed arrangement to the front counter. She had barely set it down when she halted and stared out the window. "Is that our famous writer?"

Boyd was making his way to the front door, his bodyguard at his heels. "Yes it is. And that's Eldon Landis with him." Kaylee realized Mary hadn't met Boyd, and she noticed with amusement that she was fluffing her hair and smoothing her apron. "You look fine."

"It's not every day you meet someone on the best-seller list." Mary leaned closer to the mirror over the workbench and pinched her cheeks to give them color. "I want to make a good impression."

The men entered the shop. Boyd bestowed a dazzling smile on the two women. "Good morning. Nice shop you have here." He pointed at the windows. "Love the pumpkins."

"They've been pretty popular this season," Kaylee said. She introduced Mary to Boyd and Eldon. "What's up?" she asked, hoping there wasn't any more bad news.

"Remember those curtains you mentioned?" Boyd said. "Since we were downtown, I thought I'd pick them up. Save you the trouble of hauling them over to my place."

Kaylee came around the end of the counter. "You might as well take the gun too, while you're here."

While Mary gasped and Eldon gaped, Boyd said, "I was hoping you'd say that. I'm dying to take a peek at it."

"What gun?" Mary managed to ask.

Kaylee stopped to explain, resting her hands on her hips. "I think I found Jack Butler's .38 in one of Edna's trunks. I planned to have Reese take it to Boyd but I haven't had time." She started moving again. "Follow me. Everything is in the attic."

"Why don't you wait here, Mr. Landis?" Mary offered when the other man began to follow. "How about a cup of coffee? I'm ready for a break." Bear yipped. "And someone needs his treat."

As Kaylee started up the stairs to the second floor, she heard Mary telling Eldon, "I've worked here for years, and I never knew there was a gun in the attic. This place is full of surprises."

Boyd chuckled. "Nice lady. You must enjoy working with her."

Kaylee reached the top of the stairs and headed toward the next flight. "I sure do. I inherited her from my grandmother along with this business and my home." Up in the attic, she turned on the light. "Here we are."

Boyd stared around at the belongings crammed into the large room. "Wow. There's tons of stuff in here." His voice held appreciation and excitement, not the usual reaction of people encountering an attic stuffed to the rafters.

It must be the writer and researcher in him, Kaylee reflected. "I know. I hope I can find time to go through it all someday." She picked her way over to Edna's area, warning Boyd to watch out for the hazards along the way.

First, she pulled out the box with the gun, knowing that trumped curtains any day. Boyd opened the lid and gazed at the firearm almost reverently. "J.B.'s .38." His finger traced the initials engraved into the grip. "We need a ballistics test."

"To see if it matches the bullet in Jack's body? Reese said the same thing." Kaylee opened another trunk in search of the curtains.

"Absolutely. I've learned never to assume, no matter how obvious it might seem." Boyd set the lid gently on the box. "Thank you for letting me borrow this."

"No problem. I'm as eager as you to fill in the missing pieces. And Edna's life was full of them." She found the curtains at last and pulled one out from the chest. "Do these look like yours?"

Boyd felt the fabric between two fingers. "I think so. Can we spread it out and see how long it is?"

With his help, Kaylee unfolded the bulky curtain and held it up. Kaylee scanned front and back. "It looks like it's in really good condition. It's not faded at all."

Boyd lifted it up a couple more inches. "It's heavier than it appears," Boyd said. "Is that because of the lining, do you think?"

Kaylee bent to check the hem. "Sometimes they used to sew weights in curtains to make them hang straight." She felt something hard inside the fabric. "That's odd. The weight is round, not square. Not very thick either."

"Round?" Boyd dropped the curtain, which thumped to the floor and raised a cloud of dust. "Sorry about that." He crouched down and began to pull the hem apart.

Kaylee sat back on the floor, bewildered by this sudden interest in curtain construction. She watched as he reached into the hem pocket—and pulled out a shiny gold coin.

He held it up between his thumb and forefinger, a huge grin breaking across his chiseled features. "I think we just found Lester's loot."

18

Kaylee stared at the gold coin in fascination. "Let me see." Boyd handed it to her, and she flipped it front and back, studying the images and date. The 1906 Liberty coin appeared to be in pristine condition.

Without saying another word, she began to pull at the curtain hem, joined by Boyd working from the other end. Every couple of inches, they found another coin. Kaylee placed them carefully on a scrap of fabric.

"That's one mystery solved," Boyd said. "I wonder where the paper money is."

Kaylee felt the thickness of the curtain. "I think it's inside." She tore the stitches attaching the silky inner layer to the velvet.

The entire inside of the curtain was lined with bundles of money, held in place by clever rows of stitching across the double liner. Boyd stacked them up, counting. "This is some of it. Where's the rest?"

"Maybe in the other curtains." Kaylee pulled out one, a second, then a third, but couldn't find circular weights or packets of bills in any of them. She bundled the last curtain into a ball. "Do you think Edna spent it all?"

"I doubt it," Boyd said. "According to the records I found, she died a pauper, at least officially. She was ill for a while and her business began to fail." He grabbed one of the curtains and checked it again. Light broke across his face. "I bet I know where it is. In the curtains at the cottage, where it's been for decades. Or maybe just one or two of them, since they might not have spread it out that much."

Kaylee folded the curtains and crammed them back into

the box. Then, she gathered up the money and coins in a basket. "We'd better get this to the bank," she said as she followed him through the attic. What were the rules about found money? She'd have to find out. This portion of the robbery proceeds had been discovered on her property.

As they descended the stairs, her conscience panged. How could she even consider keeping stolen money, even if the statute of limitations had run out and it was legal? Which it might not be, after all. If it did rightfully belong to her, she'd give it back or donate it to a worthy cause.

Downstairs in the showroom, Violet Moore stood at the counter paying for a wrapped sleeve of flowers. Eldon perched on a stool, watching as Mary rang up the transaction. Kaylee halted in the doorway, not wanting word about the found money to get out quite yet. But Boyd didn't have any such compunction.

"Kaylee and I have solved the mystery of the missing loot," he announced. He held up the curtain. "Edna sewed packets of bills and gold coins into the lining."

Mary was so startled she messed up the transaction and had to cancel it. "The money was here all the time?" She picked up Violet's card and swiped again.

"Well, part of it. We think the—" Boyd bit off the words when Kaylee elbowed him in the back.

She set down the basket of money on a stool. "We're not sure where the rest of it is, actually. It's a fluke that we found this."

Violet's eyes darted between the curtain and the basket, her mouth hanging open. "Oh my. I can't believe you solved the mystery. People have been wondering for decades where it went. Edna refused to say." She clapped a hand over her mouth as if she had revealed too much.

"Oh, did the Moore family look for it?" Kaylee asked. "I recently learned that Edna was related to them."

The farmer's wife shook her head. "I have no idea. I was only making an assumption. Otherwise, why would the money still be here—in a curtain, no less?"

"Very crafty of Edna, and right in keeping with her profession," Mary said. She slid the receipt across the counter so Violet could sign it. "Thanks for coming in."

Violet scrawled her name on the slip and picked up her flowers. "You bet." She nodded at the pumpkins in the window. "Love what you've done with them. Hopefully Paul will sell enough to keep the farm going." With that remark, she strode from the shop, head held high.

The onlookers were quiet until the jingling bells died away. Mary sniffed. "Nothing like setting off a bomb and making a hasty exit."

As far as Kaylee was concerned, the woman's remark shed new light on the breakup of the marriage. She'd heard financial problems were a top issue in divorce.

"I'm sorry to hear the farm is struggling," Kaylee said. "Paul does a great job and we'll keep buying from him." She lifted the overflowing basket to the counter. "Right now, I'm making a trip to the bank. I don't want this money sitting around a minute longer."

Eldon stood and gave her a crooked grin. "I'll be your bodyguard if you want. Word about that fortune is going to spread faster than soft butter on a hot biscuit."

Mary glanced at the clock. "Speaking of hot biscuits, I'll put in an order at the Pacific Street Diner. I think a celebration is called for."

"Good idea," Boyd said. "On me, of course." He reached out and let several of the shiny gold coins run through his fingers. "This book is definitely going to be a best seller."

In the end, Boyd accompanied Kaylee to the bank, where he

had her take several photos of him with the money in the safety deposit vault. Then he took a couple of her, as his assistant and coresearcher. To Eldon's chagrin, Boyd asked him to fetch lunch while they did the banking, a decision Kaylee agreed with. The less anyone knew about the specific location of the loot, the better. She had rented the box and would keep possession of the key.

They stepped out of the vault into chaos. The lobby of the small branch was filled with pushing, chattering people. Kaylee spotted Eldon in the doorway, carrying two brown sacks and trying to squeeze inside.

"What's going on?" Boyd asked the teller. "A special on toasters?"

"Toasters?" She laughed. "No, they're here to see you."

Kaylee groaned quietly when she recognized a bespectacled young man pushing to the front of the throng, a camera around his neck and a recorder in his hand. Mac Jordan, reporter for the *Puget Sound Chronicle*. "We've become a media event," she muttered.

"Mr. Parsons," Mac said, his voice almost reverent. "I understand you've found the spoils of the 1935 bank robbery." He spoke loud enough that the voices in the room gradually died down.

This time, Boyd didn't mention that they'd only found part of it. He gave the reporter his most winning smile and launched into a brief summary of the day's events. When the reporter concluded by asking if he expected to find something else, Boyd said, "In addition to Jack Butler's bones?" He gave a dramatic shudder. "I sure hope not."

The crowd, listening in rapt attention, laughed and clapped. When Boyd told them that they'd need to wait until his book came out to learn more, they dispersed.

"Thanks, Mr. Parsons," Mac said, practically dancing with glee. "It's a thrill to break this story. Besides being fascinating, it's really going to boost my profile." He waved his phone, the screen showing the newspaper's social media page. "This video I took will go viral in about two minutes I bet. The news service will grab it, then the networks will call . . ." He burbled on, listing all the outlets sure to pick up the story.

"Glad we could help your career," Boyd said wryly. "Let's get out of here, Kaylee." As they crossed the rapidly emptying lobby, he said in a low voice, "I want to go home. Now."

"Good idea." Kaylee shared the itchy anticipation she heard in his voice. If there was more money to find, they needed to do it right away, before someone else beat them to the punch.

Reese was approaching the bank as they were pushing out through the double doors. "What's going on?" he asked. "I finally gave up at the drive-through teller."

Kaylee leaned close and whispered in his ear, "We found some of Edna's money. Now we're going out to Buttercup Cottage." She raised her eyebrows. "Can you join us?"

In the end, Kaylee decided to ride with Reese, while Boyd and Eldon went ahead. Kaylee and Reese brought Mary her lunch, promising a real celebration meal soon. "I don't know what I'd do without you," Kaylee said, feeling guilty at skipping out again.

Mary gave her a push. "Go on. And call me right away if you find something." She unwrapped her lunch. "I'm going to be fine right here with my deluxe cheeseburger and fries." She tossed a fry to Bear, who snapped it up. "Bear and I will hold down the fort."

Kaylee shared a cheeseburger with Reese while they drove out to Buttercup Cottage. Unlike other trips to Madrona Grove, this felt like an enjoyable excursion. "Your truck must have the way memorized," Kaylee joked. "We've been out here so many times."

"It does," Reese replied. "I don't even have to steer." He laughed and grabbed some more fries. "As for playing hooky, it was an easy choice. Clear a drainage ditch or look for treasure? Which would you pick?"

"Well, it helps that you were working at Wildflower Cottage," Kaylee said. "You know the owner quite well."

"She pays on time. Just like her grandma."

Kaylee gave a sad smile. "I sure wish I could see her on Thanksgiving." She stared out at the landscape, each day inching closer to winter. Once December came, with its rain, ice, and snow, traveling would be hard. Despite her excitement about finding Edna's hidden riches, she felt a fog of melancholy settle over her.

Nothing counted more in life than loved ones. She was so fortunate compared to someone like Edna, who had watched her husband die in a hail of bullets. Sympathy twisted in her heart for the seamstress, who had died young and left her baby an orphan. What had happened to the child?

Reese braked, returning Kaylee's attention to the road ahead. The usually deserted Madrona Grove Road was lined with cars, brake lights flashing.

"What's going on?" Kaylee asked.

The carpenter groaned. "I'm guessing the news of the treasure has hit the airwaves. Everyone and his brother is taking a ride to check out Buttercup Cottage."

"Oh no." Kaylee picked up her phone to dial Boyd and check on how things were at the cottage. As she scrolled through the directory, Reese's phone beeped.

"Can you please see what that is?" He tossed the phone to her from its place on the console, keeping his eyes on the traffic ahead.

"It's the alarm," she said. "Someone set it off." She set his phone aside and called Boyd, hoping no one had broken into the house.

"Hello?" Boyd sounded tense. "Kaylee? We've got a situation here. Where are you?"

"Madrona Grove Road. We'll be there in a few." In response, she heard an argument in the background, then Boyd shouting that he was calling the sheriff. The phone went dead. "Oh boy. We've got trouble."

"Hang on. I'm going to pass." Reese turned the wheel so the truck entered the other lane, and they roared past a line of half a dozen cars or so. Then he expertly cut back in, able to move faster without the dawdlers ahead of them.

When they reached Buttercup Cottage, he raced up the drive. After seeing that Boyd's rental sedan was the lone car in the yard, he parked sideways so he was blocking the entrance for other vehicles. "I don't know who was trying to get in, but they must have been on foot."

As if conjured by his words, Kaylee saw two young men racing toward the woods, laughing and giving each other high fives. "There they go."

"Huh. They look pretty harmless. But stupid to try to break into a house." Reese opened the driver's side door and hopped down.

Kaylee climbed out and hurried to join him. A text from Jessica dinged on her phone: *Saw the video. Call me.* Texts from DeeDee and other friends followed. She hadn't been in the eye of a media maelstrom quite like this before, and she wasn't sure she liked it. Taking a deep breath, she silenced her phone and tucked it away.

On the front porch, they knocked. Boyd answered the door and glanced both ways to check the property. "Come on in. We've had people ringing the doorbell ever since we got back. And then those two kids tried to climb through a window."

"They're gone," Reese said. He pointed at his truck. "I parked so no one can get up here."

Boyd slapped him on the shoulder. "Good move." He stood

back and ushered them inside. Despite the public frenzy, the writer appeared calm, even energized.

"Ready to check the curtains, boss?" Eldon asked when they entered the living room. He stood near a set of double windows, which held four curtains.

"Go for it," Boyd said. "We waited for you two to get here. I thought that was only fair." He moved to another window and lifted the curtain rod to release the drapes.

Kaylee and Reese took the final window. "These are heavy," Kaylee said, her chest tightening with excitement. They laid the curtains on the floor and got to work.

Boyd gave a cry of excitement. "It's here." He held up a gold coin.

Eldon whooped and pumped his fist. "All right. We found it."

Between the curtain at The Flower Patch and three panels at the cottage, they found most of the fortune, as had been reported by the bank. About a thousand dollars or so was missing.

"Edna obviously wasn't a spendthrift," Boyd said.

"She died within months of the robbery," Kaylee said. "But I wonder if she felt guilty about spending the money. After all, it was blood money."

"That wouldn't stop me," Eldon said, chuckling. "Money was made to be enjoyed. It doesn't do anyone any good sitting inside a curtain."

Boyd leveled a cold glare at Eldon. "This money is going back to the bank, where it belongs."

Eldon's broad cheekbones reddened, but he laughed off Boyd's words. "Ah, you're no fun." He hefted several bundles of hundred-dollar bills in his hands. "I could do big things with this at the casino."

Boyd took the bundles from his hands and stowed them inside a satchel. "Let's get this in a safety deposit box this afternoon. I'll sleep better without it in the house."

"Really?" Eldon held a bundle to his cheek. "I could cuddle up to this baby." Then he laughed and tossed the bundle back into the pile. "I'm joking."

Boyd gave Eldon an assessing look but continued to stow the money in the satchel.

Uneasy, Kaylee shifted on the sofa, where she sat next to Reese. Something about Eldon didn't ring true. Then she remembered the man wasn't exactly an innocent. He was a convicted felon, just not for the crime Boyd had investigated in his book.

Boyd's phone rang on the coffee table. From where she sat, Kaylee clearly saw the name on the screen. "Boyd, it's Kathy."

He swooped down and snatched the phone up. "Kathy?" His voice trembled. "Are you okay?"

The volume must have been up on the phone because Kaylee could clearly hear the response. "If you want to see your precious Kathy alive, listen to what I tell you."

19

Boyd's hand tightened on the phone, but he managed to keep his voice calm. "What are you talking about?" He turned on speakerphone so they all could hear, then put a finger to his lips to warn them to be quiet. Reese took out his phone and set it on record, a move that earned a thumbs-up from Boyd.

A bizarre laugh echoed through the speaker. The voice wasn't distinctly male or female, and it had an eerie high-pitched sound. "How much plainer can I be? We have Kathy and you have something we want—the money from the bank robbery."

Everyone's eyes went to the pile of money on the floor. "What money?" Boyd tried to bluff.

The terrible laugh again. "Everyone knows you have it. It's been on social media."

"Okay. How do I know you have *her*? You could be lying."

"Listen."

"Help me, Boyd." Kathy's voice was clear and urgent. "Please. Give them what they want."

"Are you all right, Kathy? Did they hurt you?"

The other voice interrupted. "My, my. Your concern is so sweet. She's fine. And if you want her to stay that way . . ."

Boyd exhaled a long and shuddering sigh. "All right. Tell me what I need to do."

"Come to Blossom Island tonight at seven. Alone. No deputies."

"But I don't have a boat. And I can't operate one."

"Then your captain needs to stay on the boat, offshore. You can wade in."

"I'll be there." Boyd sighed again. "Don't hurt her. Please."

"Follow orders and she'll be fine." The caller disconnected.

Reese stopped recording. "That doesn't give us much time." He lifted his phone. "Let's call the sheriff."

"No." Boyd's tone was harsh. "You heard him. No deputies."

Eldon said quietly, "It could be a trap. They want you."

Kaylee remembered her first encounter with Ned and Flint. "They were interested in the money. They asked me about it at the farm the day I met you, Boyd. They overheard us talking about your new book."

"So they want the money *and* you." Eldon jerked a thumb toward his chest. "I gotta go along. Watch your back."

Boyd collapsed onto his chair, hunching forward. He ran both hands over his face. "Let me think."

"I still feel like we need to tell the deputies," Reese said, his voice quietly insistent.

"No!" Eldon barked. "The kidnappers will hear the boats and see their lights. You don't want to risk Kathy's life, do you?" His eyes narrowed. "I could tell you about a time—"

"We don't need to hear that right now, Eldon," Boyd said. "I have an idea."

Kaylee stood at the wheel of the *KayBea*, Reese helping her navigate. She'd never piloted the boat at night—nor had she been the captain during a life-and-death excursion. Her gaze roamed over the dash ceaselessly, checking speed, radar, and direction. The moonless, overcast night made their endeavor risky under the best conditions.

"I hope this works," she said to Reese. She was speaking equally of reaching the island and rescuing Kathy. She was glad

Bear was safely with Mary for the night, giving her one less thing to worry about.

Reese leaned closer, speaking under the hum of the engine. "Don't worry. Plan B is under way."

Kaylee started to glance back at Boyd and Eldon, seated in the stern, but caught herself. She gave a slight nod of acknowledgment.

Finally, the instruments revealed they were approaching Blossom Island. She cut the speed even further. Reese directed her to the west of the island. He and Eldon were going to use an inflatable dinghy to secretly reach the shore.

"You shouldn't have any trouble finding the beach," he said.

Her insides quivered. "I hope not." She'd only been there once, during the day. *What if I can't find it and the kidnappers hurt Kathy? What if*—her thoughts began to spiral into panic.

Reese seemed to sense her anxiety because he put his hands on her shoulders and peered into her eyes. "It will be okay. I've been here tons of times." He repeated the directions.

"Got it." Eldon was already preparing to get into the dinghy and Reese turned to follow.

Impulsively Kaylee gave him a hug. "Be careful."

He hugged her back tightly. "I will. You stay on the beach, okay?"

Kaylee didn't trust herself to say anything else, so she squeezed and then let go. She watched as the two men climbed into the inflatable boat and Boyd cast them off. They would row to another landing spot, the man-powered boat hiding their presence. From there, the plan was sketchy in Kaylee's mind, but she knew one thing for sure: She could trust Reese.

Boyd joined her at the wheel while Eldon and Reese rowed away, Reese pulling strongly on the oars. "Let's get this over with," he said. In the glow of the dash lights his face was drawn and lined. "I'm so sorry to drag you and Kathy into my mess."

"It's not like you did it on purpose. Kathy is my friend. Of course I'd try to help." Kaylee kept her eyes on Reese until the yellow boat disappeared into the night. Out here on the bay, the lights of Orcas were distant specks. She squared her shoulders and reached for the throttle. "All right. Let's go."

She repeated Reese's instructions to herself as they motored back to the south beach on Blossom Island. They entered the small bay without incident, and she cut the motor offshore, as they had been instructed.

A flashlight flared on, pointed right into their faces. "Good," a man called. "You followed instructions."

Kaylee threw an arm up to block the glare. "Can you please move the light?"

Whoever it was obeyed, the beam shining on Boyd as he brandished the satchel. Then he slipped into waders for the slog to shore. Kaylee held the bag while he slipped over the side of the boat, and after he got his footing, she handed it to him.

"See you in a few," he said. Holding the leather bag above the waves, he began trudging through the water in a wide-legged stance. The circle of light moved with him, giving an effect of a spotlight on an actor.

"Be careful, Boyd," she called.

Once he reached the shingle beach, she collapsed onto the captain's chair. Now all she could do was pray. In her mind, she pictured Boyd running back over the hill, Kathy with him. The bank loot would be gone unless the deputies caught up with the kidnappers, but who cared in light of their safety and well-being?

Kaylee opened the thermos of coffee they'd brought and poured a cup with shaking hands. The night was frigid, the bone-chilling air an omen of winter. Now that the engine was silent, she heard the swish of waves against the shore and the wind moving through the pines on the bluff.

She shivered, picturing what might be happening at the

cabin. How odd that events had come full circle to the night more than eighty years ago when Jack Butler and Lester Clayton came to this island, carrying their ill-gotten gains. Only one of them had left.

After she drank the coffee, she decided to move the *KayBea* closer to shore. Why make Kathy wade through the icy water? After releasing the anchor, she picked up an oar and poled the boat like a gondola until the bottom scraped against the gritty sand.

She hopped out and tugged it forward far enough that it wouldn't lift and drift with the tide. She considered tying the boat to a tree but abandoned that thought. They might have to make a quick getaway, and the last thing they needed to do was fumble with a rope.

Kaylee found herself pacing around the beach, wondering what was going on. She checked the time on her phone. Fifteen minutes had gone by. Wavering, she glanced between the safety of the boat and the bluff ahead.

She should sneak up and see what was happening. If there was a problem, she could call the sheriff. Obeying an instinct for self-preservation, she returned to the boat and retrieved one of the steel tools her grandfather had kept for engine repairs. She zipped it into her jacket pocket and put her phone on silent so it wouldn't give her away if a call or text came through. Then she began the hike up the trail.

The footing was rough, alternating between rocks and sand. After she slipped and almost fell flat, Kaylee took out her phone and scanned the area ahead with its light. Each time, her heart crept into her throat, and she held her breath until the conspicuous glow was extinguished again.

At the top of the rise, she stopped to get her bearings. The cabin was off to the right, down a woodland path. She took the risk of shining her light again to find the opening between the trees. Otherwise she could end up lost, floundering around in the thick undergrowth.

Laughter and voices sounded from the direction of the cabin, followed by a swinging flashlight.

Kaylee ducked behind a tree, her pulse racing. It must be the kidnappers. She crouched down in some bramble bushes, heedless of the thorns tugging at her jacket and jeans.

In the light of their flashlight, she saw two figures pulling ski masks off their heads to reveal the familiar faces of Paul and Charlie Moore. Paul carried the satchel Boyd had brought to the island.

Kaylee rocked back on her heels, shock and horror twisting in her stomach.

Charlie ran a hand through her hair. "I'm sure glad to get that thing off. I have so much fuzz in my mouth." She tossed the mask into the bushes, where it landed close to Kaylee's foot.

"Small price to pay for staying anonymous." Not seeming to notice his sister's rash move, Paul tucked his own mask in his back pocket. "Let's get out of here."

Joy broke over Charlie's face. "We did it!" she cried joyously, jumping up and down. "Now we can save the farm."

"Or sell the place and leave the island," Paul said. "Some days I would love nothing more."

"How about a warmer island? Say in the Caribbean?" Charlie threw back her head and laughed.

"Now that Violet has left me, I'm ready for that. Sun and sand, sis."

Outrage swept over Kaylee in a hot flood. She rose to her feet, tempted to step out onto the path and tell the thieves what she thought of them. With a huge effort, she managed to restrain herself. Confronting them wouldn't do any good—in fact, it would only serve to put her in danger. Let them believe they had gotten away with their crimes. Justice would descend soon enough.

First she had to find Boyd and Kathy.

After Paul and Charlie's footsteps faded away, she slipped out of the forest and headed up the path. After she passed a familiar boulder jutting into the trail, she realized the cabin wasn't much farther.

She slowed, taking one step at a time. Where was everyone? All her senses heightened as she strained to see and hear in the almost utter darkness. Slow-building dread churned in her core, tingling along her veins.

Had they—she couldn't even finish the thought.

A lighted rectangle shone in the woods. The cabin.

Kaylee heard the low rumble of voices. The rush of relief was so strong, she had to grab a tree to stay upright, though its cold bark was rougher than sandpaper.

She moved with more purpose now, not afraid to step on a twig or make noise.

Then a woman's voice cried out, a short, sharp yelp.

"What'd you do that for?" Boyd shouted.

Heedless of the uneven footing, Kaylee ran. She reached the closest window and sidled up to it. Then she peeked inside, careful to stay out of view.

Boyd and Eldon stood facing each other, Boyd's face taut with anger. In contrast, Eldon's demeanor was nonchalant, casual even. Kathy lay on the floor between them, unconscious.

Why isn't Boyd doing anything? And where is Reese? Kaylee moved her head to get a better view. Fear lanced through her middle as she saw the answer to her first question.

Eldon was pointing a gun at Boyd. "I hate to do this to you, buddy, but you and I are taking a ride to the mainland." He cocked his head. "The boys should be here anytime to pick us up."

Boyd took a step back, both hands raised. "What are you talking about?"

"Curtis hired me to come get you." With a steady hand, Eldon kept the gun aimed at the writer. "For some reason, he didn't think asking would work."

"You? Curtis—what?" Boyd's brow creased in a frown. "I thought you . . . I didn't know . . ."

The criminal gave him a pitying look. "Rookie mistake, Parsons. Just because I wasn't involved with that heist doesn't mean I wasn't part of the gang."

"Seriously?" Boyd rubbed his chin, trying to take in this new information. "I should have left you in jail to rot."

Kaylee cringed, expecting a gunshot. That remark was either brave or reckless.

"I can understand you feeling that way." Eldon lifted a shoulder. "If it's any consolation, I didn't want to do it. But Curtis called in a favor." He waved the gun. "Come on, let's go."

"What about Kathy? We can't leave her here."

Eldon regarded the woman sprawled on the floor. "I didn't hit her that hard. She'll be okay. No doubt Kaylee will get curious and find her, sooner or later."

The tool in Kaylee's pocket bumped against the siding when she moved. She'd forgotten it was there. An idea trickled into her mind. Should she? Yes. She unzipped her pocket and pulled out the tool, the metal cold in her grip.

She padded around the cabin and tiptoed up onto the porch. As she'd hoped, the two men didn't seem to hear her. Outside the open door, she stayed out of sight while she took stock of the situation.

Perfect. Eldon stood with his back to the door, his eyes fixed on Boyd. Before Boyd could spot her and give her away, Kaylee darted forward, grabbed his collar, and pressed the end of the ratchet extension against Eldon's neck.

"Drop your gun or I'll shoot." Kaylee made her voice gruff, trying to sound as if she meant it.

Boyd's mouth dropped open. When he recovered from his surprise, he gave her an almost imperceptible nod of approval.

Eldon chuckled as he tried to look over his shoulder. "Come on, Kaylee. You don't mean it. Besides, where did you get a gun?"

"Go on, drop it." Bracing her feet, Kaylee pressed on the metal tube, so it dug further into his skin. If he caught a glimpse of the harmless tool, she was doomed. "Unless you'd like to experience a bullet from a .38. This gun belonged to Jack Butler. It's already killed one man in this cabin."

"I'd do what she says, man," Boyd advised.

Kaylee could sense Eldon's thoughts whirring as he weighed options. The relaxation of his shoulders told her he'd made a decision. He tossed the gun onto the ancient chair, where it landed safely.

Boyd launched himself forward and tackled Eldon. Caught off guard, the felon fell to the floor like a sack of bricks. Boyd jumped on top of him. "There's some rope in the corner," he said, breathing heavily. "They used it on Kathy."

Kaylee dropped the tool to the floor with a clang and began looking for the rope. Along the way, she picked up Eldon's gun.

"She held me up with a ratchet?" Eldon began to laugh. "Sure you don't want a job, girl? You've got guts."

"Where's Reese?" Kaylee found the rope and dumped it beside Boyd. She leaned close to Eldon. "You better not have hurt him."

Eldon submitted while Boyd secured his hands and feet. "No, of course not. I tied him up when I found out he was in touch with the sheriff."

Reese's plan B. Kaylee's heart gave a leap. "Where is he?"

"On the west shore, near the dinghy landing."

Boyd fished around in Eldon's pocket. "You might need this." He tossed her a folded pocketknife.

Resolving to start carrying one herself, Kaylee trotted to the doorway, then halted. She'd need a real light. She grabbed one of the two flashlights in the cabin. "Take care of Kathy," she told Boyd. "And I'll go check on Reese."

"Do that." Boyd was already beside the stricken woman, who was now moving restlessly, her eyelashes fluttering. "Kathy? Can you hear me?" He gently shook her shoulder.

Kaylee flew down the path, every footstep seeming to echo Reese's name. She hoped and prayed that Eldon hadn't been lying, that he hadn't hurt her friend. Knocking Kathy out hadn't seemed to bother him at all.

Pulled high on the rocky shore, the dinghy flashed yellow in the flashlight's beam. She moved the light around the area beside it and, with a leap of her heart, spotted Reese's blue windbreaker. "Reese! Reese!" she yelled, running across the rocks to where he lay.

Careful not to blind him, she set the light down where it could reveal his features. His eyes were open and a piece of wide tape was stuck across his mouth. Grateful he was conscious and appeared unhurt, she dropped to the cold rocks beside him.

"Hang on, Reese. This might hurt." She grabbed a corner and lifted it from his skin. Sucking in a deep breath, she yanked the tape off his mouth.

"Ouch!" he hollered. "Get my hands, okay? I can't even rub my lips."

Kaylee pulled out the pocketknife and sawed at the rope around his wrists. While she worked, she filled him in on the events of the past half hour.

"You held Eldon up with a ratchet?" He gave a belly laugh. "Wow. Wish I'd seen that. You could have knocked me over with a feather when he tackled me. I thought he was one of the good guys. Good enough, anyway. He definitely had me fooled."

"He had all of us fooled," Kaylee said grimly. "I guess we expected him to be grateful to Boyd for getting him out of jail. But as they say—"

"No honor among thieves. Guess whoever coined that phrase knew what they were talking about." He sat up and rubbed his ankles.

Kaylee reflected on the irony of Eldon now being bound while Reese was free. "Now what? We have an injured woman, a captured crook, and two kidnappers on the loose."

Reese gave her a cheeky grin. "Remember what I said about plan B?" He cocked an ear and pointed skyward. The rhythmic beating of a helicopter's blades resounded across the bay. "It's now in action."

20

"Happy Thanksgiving, Bear." Kaylee smiled at her little dog, who came running into the bedroom to greet her, his tail wagging. She opened the curtains, enjoying the welcome sunshine pouring through the windows.

Bear padded after her as she went to the kitchen to make coffee. After it was brewed, she poured a cup and took a place at the table, admiring the view. Letting the coffee and sunlight warm her, she reflected on the blessings in her life. Although a week had passed since her ordeal on the island, she was still shaken by gusts of relief and gratitude at how it had all turned out.

Reese's backup plan had been to notify the deputies beforehand, who arrived by helicopter so as not to alert the kidnappers with the sound of a boat engine. Their timing had been off due to Reese's inability to call them once he and Eldon reached the island. Thankfully, Deputies Brooks and Garcia had followed up anyway.

Kaylee and Reese had explained the sequence of events and the present status of the situation. Via the helicopter radio, Deputy Brooks dispatched other deputies to intercept Paul and Charlie on their way back to Orcas. Then they went to the cabin to arrest Eldon and check on Kathy. By then, the marine patrol had arrived. Kathy was flown to the hospital to be examined and received a clean bill of health.

As for Eldon, he was promptly taken into custody and charged with a number of crimes. While he was being handcuffed, he had been unrepentant. "What are you arresting me for?" he demanded. "Miss Bleu accosted me with a deadly weapon."

Deputy Brooks had given her a questioning look, but then Boyd had burst into laughter. "He was holding a gun on me when she bluffed him with a ratchet." He pointed to the piece of metal, still on the floor where Kaylee had dropped it. "If she hadn't done that, I might be in Seattle right now." His face twisted. "Or swimming with the fishes."

Brooks read Eldon his rights and cuffed him. "No doubt he's the one who assaulted you at the house, Mr. Parsons," he said to Boyd.

"Don't pin that on me," Eldon squawked. "It was that drip, Paul Moore. I saw him do it." He explained how he'd used the incident to gain Paul's cooperation in luring Boyd into a trap, with Kathy as bait. The Moores would get the money and Eldon would get Boyd.

"You're a cagey one, Landis," a familiar voice said. Ned and Flint stood in the cabin doorway. Ned tipped sunflower seeds from a packet into his palm and tossed them into his mouth. "With your priors, you're looking at serious time."

Flint nodded at Deputy Brooks. "Thanks for arranging for marine patrol to bring us over, but it seems like everything is over but the paperwork."

"Who are you?" Kaylee blurted. Her head was spinning from this unexpected twist. She'd been so certain the bird-watchers were bad guys after Eldon told them as much.

"We're FBI, undercover," Ned said. "We got word that Landis was going to make a move against our man Parsons here. We've been tailing Landis for weeks."

"And eating sunflower seeds," Kaylee said. Everyone stared at her. "I found the hulls all over the place. In the woods, outside Boyd's house . . ."

Flint gave her a nod of approval. "I've been on his case about that. He leaves the hulls everywhere, like a trail of bread crumbs. Not so good when you're working undercover."

Ned's response was to eat another handful of seeds. "They help me think." He pointed at Eldon, talking between chewing. "If you cooperate by giving us info on Curtis, it could help you."

While Kaylee respected their need to go after bigger criminal fish, she had a few questions of her own for Eldon. "Was it you who hit my truck? Broke into my house? Stalked me in the woods?" The memory of the hooded figure watching her still made her shiver.

Eldon scoffed. "No way. That was Charlie and Paul. Check his old farm truck. I noticed it had a dinged front bumper. They were trying to discourage you from digging into the treasure hunt. And Charlie wanted to see what was in the old broad's papers you found." His lip curled. "Amateurs. Can't stand the heat, get out of the kitchen."

Even now, days later, the memory of Eldon's bravado made Kaylee shake her head. Some people might appreciate what Boyd had done for them, but not Eldon. He cared only about his own skin.

Her thoughts turned to Paul and Charlie, who had found the deputies waiting for them when they reached the Madrona Grove marina. They were caught red-handed in possession of the bank robbery proceeds, so their denials fell on deaf ears. Paul finally confessed to everything, including breaking into Wildflower Cottage and stealing Edna's papers, which meant that Kaylee wouldn't have to testify as a witness. She did point the deputies to the mask Charlie had left in the woods.

Boyd had managed to set up a jailhouse interview with Paul, and he invited Kaylee along.

"You can only talk about family history," Paul's attorney had said. "No discussion of my client's alleged involvement with the kidnapping."

"That's fine with me," Boyd said. "I want the information

for my book about the 1935 bank robbery." He switched on a recorder. "Are you ready, Paul?"

The subdued Paul nodded. "What else do I have to do today?"

Kaylee had almost felt sorry for him, but then she remembered that he had helped his sister kidnap Kathy. And before that, Charlie had lured the librarian to Boyd's in hopes that she'd be arrested.

As it turned out, Kathy had been spending a few days in a friend's seasonal home on the island when Charlie Moore came to pay a visit. Thinking Charlie was there for moral support, Kathy readily let her in. Instead, Charlie and her brother had spirited Kathy away to the cabin on Blossom Island, the site where their ancestor had killed his partner in crime.

That was the shocker Paul revealed in the jail's visiting room, the missing piece of Edna's story. "After Lester died, Edna got sick," Paul said. "Her relatives took the baby in, and that little guy was my grandfather." He glared at them. "We were owed that money. Orville Clayton cheated Lester's father out of his share in the bank. Lester only took what belonged to him. The value of his father's share, to the penny."

And he'd planned to divide that with his compatriots . . . or had he? After all, he'd ended up alone with the money on Blossom Island.

As Kaylee sat at the breakfast table drinking coffee and pondering the mystery, she shifted with discomfort. This part of the story always bothered her. While she didn't condone Lester's crimes, she admitted to a soft spot for the young man and his pregnant wife.

Thinking of Edna reminded her that she still had the vintage sewing patterns, even though the crate of Edna's papers hadn't been recovered yet. Mary's seamstress friend, Betty, was helping with the community Thanksgiving meal they'd all be sharing later that day at the Northern Lights Inn—Betty was one of the mashed potato brigade—so Kaylee figured she should take them to her.

Before Kaylee gave away the patterns, however, she wanted to look through them again. The old-fashioned styles were quaint and rather feminine, certainly worth admiring. She refilled her coffee cup and went to the living room where the patterns were still sitting on a shelf. She studied the designs one by one, wondering how it would be to wear a dress every day. The 1930s were a time of defined waists, with full skirts and puffed or long sleeves. The more formal outfits included gloves and hats. The evening gowns were divine. Kaylee especially liked one with a plunging back, a modest square neckline, and diamond insets in the bodice and skirt.

With a pang, she noticed the last one was for a baby's christening outfit. Had Edna made her baby's gown from this pattern? It had definitely been used, judging by the ripped envelope and the haphazard way the pieces were stuffed inside. As she fiddled with the package, several lined pages fell out.

Thinking they were notes, she unfolded them for a quick glance. What she read gave her a jolt. At the top of the page was a December date in 1935. The letter was addressed to Maisie Fitz, and the last page was signed by Edna Taylor Clayton.

Kaylee sucked in a breath of excitement and began to read.

Dearest Maisie,

We haven't spoken since the events of this fall. That's understandable since almost no one else is talking to me either. But as my dearest friend, I wanted you to know the truth about that fateful day.

I am writing this letter from my sickbed, where I fear

I won't linger much longer, so please set aside your dismay and anger and give me a fair hearing.

I am dying. The doctor didn't say so, but I know the signs. My mother had pneumonia too, and once it grips our fragile lungs, there is no reprieve this side of heaven.

Lester was a good man. I know it's a strange thing to say about a bank robber. But we are all sinners, are we not, and though I don't make excuses for his crime, it doesn't ruin his entire character. We were married already when he told me about his plan. No matter how hard I tried to talk him out of it, I couldn't dissuade him.

But I don't write this to plead his cause. That is in the hands of a higher Judge now. Lester and his family were impoverished by his uncle, who forced Lester's father out of his bank position. His father killed himself as a result, leaving the family in even more dire straits. Lester vowed revenge.

He stole back only the amount of money his uncle stole from his father. He was to come get me and we were going to flee to Canada, where one of his friends had relatives.

So far, this concurred with what Kaylee knew. She paused to take a sip of her rapidly cooling coffee. According to the mantel clock, she'd better get started baking soon. She planned to contribute a large pan of bread pudding with pumpkin and cranberries to the community dinner, and she had to get it done before Reese came to pick her up. She was torn, but curiosity told her she had to finish this letter first, so she read on.

The day of the robbery, I was waiting, my bag packed and a little christening outfit and layette prepared for our babe. I went about my business the best I could, knowing that it would be evening before I saw Lester.

He and the others were going to wait on Blossom Island until nightfall. Then they were to come and get me, and we would sail for Canada.

The hours went by in an agony of suspense and fear. I knew that something could go wrong any moment. The men might not even make it out of the city. If they were arrested, I wouldn't know until the next day, when the papers came out.

Finally, around midnight, the knock came on my door. But when I opened it, a glad smile on my lips and joy in my heart, I got the worst shock of my life.

Jack Butler stood there. He was so similar in height and build and even face structure to Lester that for a long, dizzy moment, I thought I was seeing things. The two of them used to be called the Gold Dust Twins when they played pool and cards.

Both were so lucky. Until now. I stood back and let him enter—a huge mistake, but I was in shock. "Where's Lester?" I asked.

He swaggered in, thumbs in his belt. "Lester isn't going to make it."

When I screamed, demanding he tell me why, he said that Lester was killed in an accident on Blossom Island.

Kaylee gasped so loudly, Bear lifted his head from where he lay in front of the fireplace. "It's okay, Bear. Something I'm reading." She had to pause for a few seconds to let this new information sink in. The body on Blossom Island must be Lester. Had Jack put his ring on Lester's finger? It explained why Edna had Jack's gun. She kept reading.

> *Jack said he had come to take care of me for Lester, that he planned for the authorities to believe Lester's body was his, that we would go to Canada as planned. I told him I would rather die. He told me to reconsider that. Meanwhile, did I have any food for him?*

> *I fed him after he stashed the treasure under some loose floorboards, cursing him silently all the while. He fell asleep soon after, on the couch where Lester had proposed to me. By now, the news had spread from Seattle and there was a manhunt on. Two of the robbers had been captured down near the mainland docks.*

> *Working faster than I thought possible, the sheriff mounted a posse and came to Buttercup Cottage. They demanded Jack release me and surrender, but he foolishly refused. A gunfight ensued.*

> *Jack had more than one gun. Three actually. In the confusion of the fight, I found the one engraved with his initials. I held it for what felt like hours, but was probably only moments, considering. Should I trust the lawmen outside to protect me from a foe already in my home, who had betrayed and murdered my husband, planning to exchange identities? Or did I risk him kidnapping me and my unborn child—all*

I had left of Lester—and living out the rest of my days with the despicable man who had ruined my life?

It was not a fate I would accept for Lester's child, to be raised by his murderer.

When Jack wasn't looking, I raised the gun, aimed it, and pulled the trigger. The weapon bucked in my hands, and Jack crumpled to the floor.

The deputies never knew it was me, not them, who ended the fight. I am horrified that I have taken a life, but I had no other choice. I know I will pay for this sin as well as my others after I pass.

I've made arrangements for my son, Gerald, to go to my relatives after I'm gone. They will raise him well and provide for him. I've asked them to use their last name, Moore, for him, so that his life is not darkened by his father's choices. People will not understand, and I don't want that to affect him.

Someday he will find the fortune I have stashed away for him in some of my curtains. I would like him to share it with those who bring him up as some small repayment for what they have done for me in agreeing to care for my most precious treasure.

Now you know my secrets, dear friend. Please forgive me.

Love,

Edna

Kaylee leaned back in her chair with a sigh, mulling over the tragic story. Apparently poor Edna had died before she'd found the courage to send this letter. Later today she would share it with Boyd, who would be thrilled at the discovery of another missing piece of Edna's story.

When all was said and done, Kathy and Boyd had decided they were better off as friends. Although Kathy only dated Ned once or twice, the pleasure of his company had made her realize that it truly was over between her and Boyd.

As for Violet, she'd filed for divorce from Paul and had moved to the mainland in a rush. No surprises there. Kaylee heard that she'd gotten a great job managing a large perennial nursery.

The phone rang, interrupting her reverie. She smiled when she saw the name on the display. "Happy Thanksgiving, Reese," she answered. She was looking forward to sharing the meal with him—and yes, even trying his oyster stuffing.

"Happy Thanksgiving to you too." He sounded slightly distracted, and she heard the clank of dishes in the background. He must be cooking. "I was wondering, can I pick you up a little early? Jess needs me to grab something on the way to the dinner."

Kaylee checked the time. "Give me an hour, okay? I've got to make my pudding." Not to mention shower and dress. She jumped up from the chair and headed to the kitchen while still on the phone. She and Reese agreed on the new time and, after they hung up, she flew into action.

An hour later on the dot, she stood by the front door, dressed in cranberry-colored slacks and a cream sweater, her still-warm pan of pudding in an insulated carrier.

When Reese pulled in, she said goodbye to Bear and hurried to the truck. After greeting him and stowing the pudding next to his pan of stuffing—which smelled amazing—she asked, "What are you picking up?"

"I'm not sure. Something at the Tortoiseshell Hotel."

"Oh, I bet it's something good," Kaylee said. "They have wonderful food." No doubt the loss and subsequent arrest of their previous manager, Charlie Moore, was demoralizing. But the place was so special, she was sure it would survive.

"I'm sure it is," Reese agreed. "It will only take us a minute out of our way."

They pulled up in front of the hotel. Kaylee was gratified to see a few of The Flower Patch's decorative pumpkins out on the front porch.

"Why don't you come in with me?" Reese asked when he cut the engine. "There might be a lot."

"Sure thing." Kaylee opened the door and slid out. She followed him into the lobby. At first, her attention was absorbed by the Thanksgiving displays set up throughout the space. Then the pleasant, infectious sound of a woman laughing caught her ear. Just listening to it made her feel warm and fuzzy, almost nostalgic.

She looked in that direction and saw two elderly women sitting on a love seat together. Their obvious pleasure in each other's company made her smile.

As she walked across the gleaming wood floor, her steps faltered. She blinked, not sure if she was seeing things. Could it be—?

One of the women turned to face her. "Happy Thanksgiving, dear." Bea beamed.

"Surprise!" the other lady said. It was Bea's twin sister, Lucille.

In tandem, the twins stood and strolled across the lobby toward their granddaughter and great-niece. Kaylee threw a glance at Reese, who was standing nearby, grinning. "Did you know about this?"

"I never said I was picking up food," he said. "You made that assumption."

Kaylee, engulfed in perfume-scented hugs, gave way to a fit of giggles. The last couple of weeks had been full of surprises, many of them unpleasant. This was one she welcomed. "Happy Thanksgiving," she said. "Now let's go eat."